For My Good:
The Prequel

TANISHA STEWART

For My Good: The Prequel

Copyright © 2019 Tanisha Stewart

Books may be purchased in quantity and/or special sales by contacting the publisher, Tanisha Stewart, by email at tanishastewart.author@gmail.com.

Cover Design: Tyora Moody
www.tywebbincreations.com

First Edition

Published in the United States of America
by Tanisha Stewart

Dedication and Acknowledgments

First and foremost, I dedicate this book to my Lord and Savior Jesus Christ. Without Him, I would not be here today.

Secondly, I would like to dedicate this novella to my family and friends. To my mother, Alice Jenkins, my beloved "Alice Jean," the driving force behind most of my life's accomplishments, you have been there through thick and thin, through good and bad, through struggle and triumph. Words cannot express how thankful and grateful I am for you. To my little sister, my "favorite girl" Goleana Grant, thank you for always supporting me. I am your biggest fan!

To my brothers James Auston, Thomas Stewart, Arthur Caldwell, and James Stewart, I love you all, and I thank you for supporting me in my endeavors. To my grandmother, Sue Stewart, thank you for your wisdom and your sense of humor, and for always encouraging me. To my father, James Stewart Jr., I love you, and I thank you for your constant encouragement and inspiration. To all of my extended family and friends, God bless you all. I dedicate this to you.

To my cover designer, Tyora Moody of Tywebbin Creations, for your excellent work. I am constantly in awe of your designs and how after only one email, you "get" the vision.

Next, I would like to dedicate this book to all of my high school and college students past, present, and future. You guys wake me up every morning and keep me on my feet throughout the day. I love you all, and I thank you for inspiring me in your own unique ways.

I also cannot forget to mention my alpha readers and review team. God bless each and every one of you. You help to develop me as an author, and you provide critical feedback regarding each story I write. I look forward to hearing from you with every published work.

Last but certainly not least, I dedicate this book to you, the reader. Without you, no one would hear the stories being told. I pray that this book will bless you, and that God will be glorified in and through your life. In Jesus's name, Amen.

Table of Contents

For My Good:
The Prequel

TANISHA STEWART

Prologue

Gina

"Good morning, beautiful," Kayden Senior said.

Today was our third anniversary. Kayden had left out at about five o'clock this morning to do some overtime for his job. He worked at a telecommunications company and had just recently finished his third interview for a supervisor position. We were hoping and praying he would get it, because then we could finally get married and buy a house that our baby, Kayden Junior, could grow up in.

"Good morning, sexy. Happy Anniversary," I responded, wiping sleep from my eyes.

"You too. Kayden still sleep?"

I looked over at the crib.

"He sure is. He's such a good baby."

"I know he's good. Just like his daddy."

I chuckled. "You right about that. How is work? What time you getting off?"

"I'm only working til 12 today, but I want to take you out somewhere nice tonight. They are supposed to give me the call today, and I want us to go out and celebrate."

My jaw dropped. "They are calling today?" *That would be a great anniversary gift!*

"Yup. For some reason, they like to do their calls on Friday nights after regular business hours. I guess it makes sense because if they let you know during your shift, it could mess with your head that you didn't get it. But I was told by one of the secretaries that she heard that I was the most promising candidate."

My heart swelled with pride for my man. "Ohh… Baby, I am so proud of you! Omg - I gotta go get a dress."

"Yes, buy something sexy. And ask your mom if she can watch Kayden overnight tonight. I might need you all to myself."

I blushed. "I'll do that. You can have whatever you like."

"Whatever I like?"

"Yes."

"Don't get me started girl. I'll come home right now."

"Come on. He's still asleep."

He chuckled. "You stay tempting me. But let me get off this phone. I'll see you when I get off."

"Okay. See you soon."

"Love you."

"Love you too."

After I hung up with Kayden, I went ahead and called my mom to ask if she could keep Kayden Junior all day and overnight. I needed to go get my hair and nails done, and get me a sexy dress, just like Kayden asked for. I knew just the one I would get too. I had been eyeing it for a while.

I wonder if he's going to propose?

For some reason, that question popped in my mind.

He had been hinting at it for a while, and I kind of had the feeling that he was just waiting until the promotion went through to make sure we would be more financially stable. I mean, sure he made good money with his current position, but as a supervisor, he would be next in line for even higher paid management promotions as well. If that secretary was right and he got a favorable call tonight, we would make enough to allow me to be a stay at home mom, which was what we both wanted.

Our current situation involved me doing that, but we weren't living as comfortably as we would like.

Oh well - I couldn't wait til tonight.

I picked up the phone to tell my girl Melanie the great news.

Keisha

I could not believe what I had just done.

"Keisha?" My mom was saying. "Did you hear what the doctor said?"

"Yes, I heard him," I said, but I barely felt like I was there.

They were about to discharge me. I would have to go out and face the real world.

My mom studied my expression. "They arrested him, girl. You have nothing to worry about. You saw them take him out in handcuffs."

"Yeah, but he could already be bailed out by now."

Tears clouded my vision as it really started to hit me.

He was going to kill me when he got out.

"Keisha, you will have to face that battle when it comes. There might be a trial, but you have proof of your injuries. He's not going to have a leg to stand on in court. His ass is going down, and if he comes anywhere near you, I got Smith & Wesson on speed dial. He can mess around if he wants to."

My mom looked like she was ready to shoot Rico.

Like she longed for him to try to approach me while she was there, so she could send him to his maker.

"Mom, but what about when I go to work? He knows my schedule. What if he waits there til I get off?"

This was quickly becoming a nightmare.

Rico had done all that and more. He popped up on me at my job all the time, screaming on me in the parking lot in front of customers and coworkers and everything. It was a wonder that I hadn't been fired.

And now that I had told…

I grimaced at the thought of what he would do to me when he got out.

"Keisha?" My mom called my name again, but I was in and out of focus.

"I can't leave this hospital, Mom. This is the only place I'm safe."

"No, it's not. You can get the locks changed to your apartment. We already talked to the landlord, remember?"

I began trembling. "But Mom, the windows are still low. What if he kicks one in? What if I get home and he's already there? He's going to kill me."

"Keisha, you stop that right now!" My mom gave me a stern look.

When she saw that I was halfway out of my mind, her expression softened.

"This is what we are going to do: You are going to sign your discharge papers. We are going to see if your job can transfer you to another location. We'll have your landlord change your locks, and in the meantime, you can stay at my place until you feel comfortable enough to go back home."

I sniffled as I stared blankly into space.

"Look at me," my mom said.

I couldn't.

She made everything she was saying sound so easy, but she wasn't the one with the target on her back.

"Look at me," she repeated. She gently grabbed my chin and turned my head to face her.

A tear rolled down my cheek, and she wiped it away.

"Keisha. You are down, but not out. You are not going to let that man take your dignity. You are going to walk with your head held high, and you are going to get through this. Just lean on Jesus, like I have been telling you, Keisha. You are not the first woman to fall for some punk who thinks it's okay to put his hands on a woman. You have a Momma who knows how to pray, and a Heavenly Father who never slumbers nor sleeps."

We just stared at each other til I felt myself start to calm down.

"Plus I got my Glock."

That caused us both to laugh.

I finally felt okay to leave.

Melanie

I wiped the tears from my face as I stared in the mirror.

It had only been a few months since I broke things off with Jarvis, but the pain still hit deep.

How could a man claim that he loved you, yet go and sleep with some random bitch?

I really thought that me and Jarvis was meant to be together forever. But nope.

He was just like these other slimy ass niggas. Couldn't keep his dick in his pants.

I opened myself up to him completely, and he just trampled on my heart like I meant nothing.

And of course, he did it after we already had our son, so now I was tied to him for life anyway.

He steady blowing up my phone trying to get me back, but I really don't want shit to do with him.

If it wasn't for our son, he would never see me again.

He waited til right before Jeremiah's first birthday to tell me he had been creeping with some dusty bitch named Roxanne.

I looked her up on social media after I left his apartment and went to my mom's house.

Bitch ain't have shit on me.

Fuck was he thinking?

Apparently, he wasn't, and that's why he is trying to get me back. But I don't care. He will never have the chance to put me in that position again.

I done already moved on and found me a few new men.

First Tray from my job. He worked security, while I worked at one of the clothing stores in the mall. He walked me to my car one night, and I let him come through later that evening.

It was supposed to be a one night stand, but he was cute, so I let it stick.

Then it was Marvin. I met him at the club. He was kind of corny, but I was feigning for affection at the time so I let him hit too. He's been calling me ever since.

Then I met Kylon and I felt something different.

He didn't even ask me for sex at all when we first started talking. We still haven't even slept together yet.

The more I talk to him, the more I like him, but I'm still seeing Tray and Marvin, so I told him I wanted to take it slow.

My phone rang, shaking me out of my thoughts. It was my bestie, Gina.

"Hey Boo!" I sang into the phone.

"Hey Girl. Guess what?"

"What?"

"Kayden is expecting his job to call him, and he says he wants to take me out somewhere real nice tonight."

My jaw dropped. "For real? Yass, girl! Congratulations! Happy anniversary, too. Do you think he is finally going to propose?"

"Thank you, and I think so, girl. He told me to pull out all the stops."

"Okkkayyy, get it, Baby! Gina bout to get her a ring, Honey!"

"I mean, I don't know for sure yet, but my gut tells me I'm right."

"Wow, I am so happy for you, Gina." I smiled. "I know how long you have been waiting for this."

"I know. Thank you. I'm about to get my hair and nails done, then there is this dress I have been eyeing for a while. Wanna come?"

Hell yeah! Girl, we bout to have you looking like you was sent from Heaven, Baby!"

Gina laughed. "Girl, you are too much. I'm on my way over your house."

I hung up with Gina with my spirits completely lifted.

Despite the bullshit I had going on, at least one of us was happy.

***

Gina and I went and got our hair and nails done, then we got her dress, shoes, and accessories. Kayden was not going to be able to keep his hands off of her tonight, that's for sure.

I couldn't wait to hear the details of his proposal later, with my vicarious living ass.

I shot her a text later that evening joking that she better not be making no more babies.

She shot me a text back saying she wasn't making any promises. I could tell she was souped.

Jeremiah was with Jarvis for the weekend, and all of my men were still at work, so I decided to take a nap.

I went to sleep thinking good thoughts about Gina and Kayden, but about an hour later, I woke up to a very shocking phone call.

"Melanie!" Gina screamed through the phone.

"What? Gina, what's wrong?" I looked at the clock. Literally only an hour had passed since we last texted each other. What the hell could have happened that fast?

"Melanie…" She said, her voice lower, but I could tell she was breaking down.

All types of thoughts were swirling in my mind. *Omg, Lord - please not the baby. Did something happen to Kayden? Why is she breaking down like this?*

"Gina, I need you to tell me what happened, okay?"

"Kayden cheated."

My heart dropped. I felt fire brewing in the middle of my chest.

"What do you mean, he cheated?"

"Some bitch just called his phone. He left the house."

"What bitch?" Tears rushed to my eyes. There was no way my best friend was basically re-living what I had just went through with Jarvis a few months ago.

"Hold on," Gina said, then I heard noise through the phone like she was rushing to get somewhere.

I heard sounds after that like she was vomiting into the toilet.

It almost made me vomit myself.

She got back on the phone a few moments later while the toilet was flushing.

"Hello?" she said, and she sounded so miserable. My heart broke for her.

"Gina, I'm coming over, okay?"

I grabbed up my purse as I slipped on some flip flops.

"I'm on my way."

TANISHA STEWART

For My Good: The Prequel

TANISHA STEWART

Keisha

I made my way slowly through the grocery section of Walmart, trying to find the rice cakes. They usually were in aisle thirteen, but it looked like they rearranged some of the sections when they recently remodeled the place.

I briefly touched my head scarf, making sure it was still in place.

I know people would probably call me ghetto or ratchet for wearing it out in public, but today, it was the best I could do. Some days I could barely get myself out of bed, and today happened to be one of them.

"Guess that's what trauma does to you," I breathed as I made my way down yet another aisle.

Thankfully, the rice cakes were there – only they were being blocked by two females who were standing in the aisle with their shopping carts, laughing and talking up a storm.

I immediately felt myself tense up when I saw that it didn't look like they were moving any time soon.

"Girl, I told you!" said one of them, a pretty light skinned girl. Her hair and makeup were so on point, it made me feel even more self-conscious. I looked at the other girl. She was brown skinned, and also well put together, only she wasn't wearing any makeup.

I cleared my throat before I mustered up the courage to speak. "Um, excuse me?"

They stopped talking and looked at me. The one with the makeup on looked me up and down. "Yes?" she asked.

The brown skinned girl nudged her. "Melanie…" she said gently, then shot me a smile. "What's up?"

"Um, I was just trying to get to the rice cakes." I pointed at where they were next to her.

"Oh, sure! What flavor!" said the girl, bending down to get one for me.

My face flushed with embarrassment. I wasn't expecting her to do all that.

"Um, the regular ones are fine."

She quickly grabbed one and handed it to me.

"Thank you," I said, looking down at first, then forcing myself to meet her eyes.

"What's your name?" she said. "I'm Gina." She extended her hand, and I shook it.

I was taken aback. "Keisha." *Why does she want to know my name?*

"Keisha? Oh, that's pretty!"

"Thank you," I stammered. I wanted the floor to open up and swallow me.

"I'm Melanie," said the other girl, who had been assessing me the whole time.

I shook her hand too.

We made a little small talk, then went our separate ways.

They were nice, I thought to myself as I went through the other aisles to get my remaining items.

As I made my way toward the other end of the humongous store, I heard music. It was getting louder and louder with each step. Then I saw a banner and a set of speakers with a DJ standing at them. The banner read, *Grand Re-Opening Celebration!*

I wrinkled my nose as I understood.

I guess the store wanted to show off all of their new renovations, so they were playing some up to date music.

I went to one of the checkout lanes and stood in line.

Keisha and Melanie came over and got in the lane next to mine. They smiled at me, then Melanie's eyes lit up as Cash Money Records' song "Back That Thang Up" started playing.

"Ginaaaaa!" she said.

"You better not!" said Gina.

"Girrrl, listen."

Melanie left Gina standing in line as she dipped over to where the DJ was and started twerking.

Gina looked at me in embarrassment. "Oh my gosh," she said. "I swear, I can't take her nowhere."

Melanie looked like she was having the time of her life. "Come on, Gee! Fuck it up. Don't leave me hanging!" She urged Gina to come join her as she continued to twerk.

Gina looked at me, then back at Melanie.

"She always getting me into something. But I can't leave my girl hanging though."

Gina went over and started dancing too. A couple of guys jumped in behind them, and it turned into an impromptu jam session. Gina looked at me. "Come on, Keisha, what you got?" She gestured toward a third guy who looked like he wanted to dance too.

I stared at them for a few moments, having fun.

My anxiety levels shot up.

Then, I don't know what came over me. It was as if my body took a mind of its own.

I walked over to the guy and started dancing on him. I was a little shaky at first, but thankfully, he danced with me.

Before I knew it, we were all into the song.

I looked at the crowd as we danced. A few more people joined in, and others pulled out their cell phones to record. When the song was over, the crowd that had formed erupted in applause. I was smiling so hard – something I hadn't done in a long time.

The more we danced, the more free I felt.

Gina, Melanie, and I were all out of breath when the song was over. So were the guys we danced with.

"Girl, we gotta do this again sometime!" said Melanie. "What's your number?"

Gina, Melanie, and I exchanged numbers and agreed to hang out the next weekend.

Gina

I pulled into a parking space in front of the daycare and sighed.

I glanced at my son, Kayden Junior, through my rearview mirror. Although I couldn't see his face because his car seat was facing the back of the vehicle, I could tell that he was still asleep.

A tear rolled down my cheek.

"I promised myself I wasn't gonna do this today," I said as I wiped it. I was bringing my son to daycare for the first time today - thanks to his no good daddy, Kayden Senior.

How does Melanie get through it? Melanie had been bringing Jeremiah to daycare since he was three months old. I don't know how she could leave her baby like that. I mean, I know many women do it all the time, and their kids turn out just fine, but this is really hurting me that I have to bring Kayden here now.

I wanted to stay at home with Kayden until he was school age, or at least until he could talk, but Kayden Senior ruined that for me.

It's funny how your entire life can change in the blink of an eye. It seemed like just yesterday, we were happy and in love. I really thought he was going to propose.

Then, all of a sudden, life swooped in like a bitch and stole my man and my financial security, and my heart got trampled on, all in the same weekend.

He wasn't dead or anything, though I wished he was sometimes. Nope, he was just a lying, cheating bastard like many men are.

"I gotta get him in here," I breathed as I finally unclicked my seatbelt.

I was supposed to be dropping Kayden off before I went to work, but I had been dreading this day. This was my first day at the job. My mom had been supporting both my household and hers since Kayden Senior left us high and dry.

It probably would have been easier just to give up my apartment and move in with her, but I didn't want to put more burden on her. I'm grown. I should be able to figure shit out myself.

So now I'm starting this bullshit ass call center job, and putting my son in daycare. Thankfully, I was able to get a voucher for the daycare quickly. I was also on food stamps, but I couldn't bring myself to sign up for subsidized rent. Too much pride, I guess.

I slowly exited my vehicle and closed the driver side door before I made my way around to the rear passenger side where Kayden was buckled in. I stared at him through the window before I opened the door to get him out. I grabbed his little bag of necessities that I packed the night before, then picked Kayden up, careful to watch for his head because he was still sleeping.

I trudged up to the door of the place. I had done my research. They were supposed to be one of the best daycares in the area.

"Hello!" The director greeted me with a friendly smile. "Look who's ready for his first day!" She smiled at Kayden. I mustered up a half smile of my own to be polite. She led me to the infant room where Kayden would be with the other kids his age.

I felt my heart sinking with every step.

I don't want to leave him here! My heart screamed, but my mind and body pushed me forward.

When we got to the room, Kayden's teachers, Lisa and Annette immediately greeted us. That made me feel a little bit better.

It was at that moment that Kayden woke up. He looked at his teachers, then at me, then started crying.

His little tears gripped my heart. *I can't leave him here!* My heart screamed once again. But I knew I had to. I gently removed his little coat, hat, and mittens, and handed them to Lisa, willing myself not to cry. Annette was giving me a soothing smile. She must have read my expression, despite my brave front.

I stood Kayden on his feet. He was still gaining strength in his legs, but he could walk a little.

Just then, Jeremiah shot over to me. "Tee! Tee!" That was what he called me. His little toothless grin warmed my heart. At least my baby would have a friend here.

I swallowed, then I greeted Jeremiah. "Hey!"

He looked at Kayden. "Kay…" He said slowly, like he was trying to sound out his name.

"Yup! Kayden!" I encouraged him. Kayden smiled at Jeremiah, then looked up at me. I could tell he was a little afraid. Despite the fact that he and Jeremiah knew each other, this environment was still all new to him.

"How about we introduce you to some of our toys!" Lisa knelt down to Kayden's level, looking at him first, then at me. I took a deep breath and nodded.

She gently took hold of Kayden's little hand and led him and Jeremiah to the toys. Jeremiah was bursting with joy. Kayden looked unsure of himself. He picked up one of the toys and started playing with it, then he looked back at me, that unsure expression still in his little eyes.

I nodded to encourage him, fighting my eyes not to well up with tears. He gained a little more confidence, seeming to feed off of Jeremiah a little bit.

I knew it was time for me to go.

If I was going to pay these bills, I couldn't be late to orientation.

I said goodbye to the teachers, waved at Kayden and blew him a kiss, then I walked out of the playroom. I walked as confidently as I could to my car, trying to keep my head held high.

Once I got inside, all bets were off.

Thank God I saved some of those napkins from Dunkin Donuts.

Melanie

I was sitting in the employee area taking a 15 minute break when I got a text from Gina. I knew it was coming before she even sent it.

Mel… she wrote.

"Oh Lawd, lemme call this girl." I shot a glance at the clock. I still had seven minutes left, so I went to my contacts and tapped her name.

"Hello?" She answered, sounding totally devastated.

"Hey Gee. How did it go?"

"I can't leave him there, Melanie," she sniffled.

I put on the most soothing voice I could muster. "Gina… he's going to be okay. Jeremiah is there too, remember? They are really good. This is just the first day blues."

"How do you do this every day?"

I paused. I couldn't be totally honest with her, because my reaction to bringing my son to daycare was nowhere near as emotional as hers, but still, she was my best friend, so I wanted to sympathize. "Girl, it will get better day by day. Just take your time."

She sniffled again. "I guess so."

"Where are you at?"

"At the parking lot of my job." Her voice cracked. "I barely made it here."

"Gee, listen baby. It's going to be okay. I need you to wipe your tears, get your focus, and bang out this orientation. Think about it like this: you only have to be there four hours today. After those four hours, you can fly over there and get Kayden. He will be in your arms again. Hell, I get off at the same time as you, so we can even take the boys out to Chucky Cheese."

I hoped I sounded convincing. I knew this would be an emotional day for Gina. She was really attached to Kayden Junior.

"You're right," she finally responded. "It's only four hours."

I smiled, though I knew she couldn't see me. "You'll make it."

"You on break?" Her voice sounded slightly more confident now.

"Yup. I got about two minutes left. I'm gonna bang out these last few hours, then we can pick up the boys. Meet you there?"

"Yeah," she sighed. "Well, let me get in here girl, before I get fired on my first day."

"You betta not, bih!" I teased. "We mommas got bills to pay."

My phone buzzed in my ear with a text message. I took the phone away from my ear and quickly glanced at it. I smiled when I saw that it was Kylon, this guy I had been seeing. Among a few others.

"Alright girl," Gina was saying, sounding like she had a little pep in her step.

"Okay. Talk to you later."

We hung up, and I quickly responded to Kylon before heading back in to resume my shift.

Keisha

I made sure I checked all my windows to ensure that they were locked, along with my front and back doors before making my way to my bedroom. When I got inside, I propped a chair underneath the door knob to make sure I was safely locked inside before grabbing my night clothes from off my bed and going to the bathroom to take a shower.

This was my nightly ritual since I moved back into my apartment.

Since I left Rico.

Even though he was currently locked up, I never felt like I was careful enough. They had only given him a few months, so he actually could be getting out any day now.

The thought of it made me shake with fear.

Let me back up a little: Rico is my ex-boyfriend.

As you can probably imagine, he liked to put his hands on me.

But it wasn't even me that made the final decision to press charges on him - it was my mom.

The last time he hurt me, he put me in the hospital.

Rico showed up while my mom was trying to convince me to tell the police officer what he had done. Once I saw how he was looking at me, and heard my mother telling me that if I didn't end it now, he would kill me, I knew what I had to do.

I told.

So he's in jail now, but like I said, it's not for long.

I stepped into the shower and saw the steam rising all around me.

The tears began to cascade down my cheeks as I released all the pent up emotions on the inside of me.

I felt like I didn't know how to be normal.

I didn't know how to be free.

Look at me - checking and triple-checking doors and windows, propping up a chair to lock my bedroom door… When will this all end? When will it be over?

I sighed and wiped my tears as I washed my body.

Then my mind started to go to brighter things.

I had recently started going to church with my mom, something she had been on me about ever since

I left Rico. Of course, when we were together, he didn't want me going anywhere without him except work - and even then, he would pop up on me there - so church was out of the question.

But I recently started going with my mom, and honestly, it was working wonders. I really felt like God was speaking to me through the Pastor.

His words were so inspiring that I actually went and purchased a study Bible he recommended for us. I had started reading from Genesis, and the stories were so amazing.

I lathered myself up for a second time with my lavender body wash. The scent was so relaxing. It was the only thing that would help calm me down when I was feeling anxious.

Going to church wasn't the only bright thing in my life - I had really had fun with Gina and Melanie the other day at Walmart.

It felt so good to dance again.

I always loved to dance, but when Rico and I got together, it's like he sucked all the life out of me.

I barely danced when we were together.

I turned the shower water off and wrapped myself in a towel.

Maybe Gina and Melanie and I will end up being friends.

I smiled at that thought, but then I saw my reflection in the mirror.

I inspected my features.

Gina and Melanie were so pretty.

Rico was always finding something wrong about me.

My nose was too wide.

I needed to lose weight.

I never did anything with my hair.

The list went on and on.

I shook my head to bring myself out of those thoughts.

I wasn't going to let memories of Rico ruin the little bit of good I had going on in my life.

Gina

I pulled up to the daycare on Friday to pick up my son.

It had been a rough first week, to say the least.

I am not cut out for working at a call center.

And leaving my son at this place was traumatic as fuck.

On the first day, it was mostly me breaking down crying.

By day two, my baby had got the picture that I would be leaving him with these people and not staying with him throughout the day.

He literally clung to me and would not let me go.

He was screaming and looking at me like I betrayed him.

I felt like I did.

He couldn't really talk, but he was saying, "Ma! Ma! Ma!" over and over again. I knew he was calling me.

When I tell you I broke down… I broke DOWN.

How the hell do other women do this?

Days three and four were no better at all.

The staff at the daycare took it in stride though. They tried to reassure me by telling me that it was going to be okay, that other kids go through this transition period too, and that Kayden would be just fine by Friday.

Melanie tried to reassure me too, but I couldn't shake my feelings of guilt.

That guilt turned into anger and bitterness toward Kayden's father.

I was supposed to be a fucking stay-at-home mother. Not because I'm lazy, but because I wanted to stay with my son. I wanted to be his teacher. I wanted to be his primary nurturer.

Now these daycare workers are going to see my son more than me.

I shook my head and wiped my angry tears.

I was being a little dramatic - I knew it.

But I felt like life was just not fair to me.

I treated Kayden Senior like he was the king of our castle when we were together.

He shitted on me.

I can't stand his fucking ass.

I got out the car and slammed the door.

Then I realized that I needed to calm down.

I couldn't go in this place with a nasty attitude.

They were really working hard with my son, and I didn't want him to see his mommy unhappy.

I wanted him to have the best childhood ever, despite my problems.

I fixed my face and put some pep in my step as I entered the building.

I was immediately greeted by Monica, the director.

"Hey, how are you?" she smiled, and I smiled back.

"I'm good. Just finishing my first week of orientation at my new job."

"Oh? How was it? Do you like the job?"

I fought back a grimace. "It's okay. I just have to get used to it."

"Well, Kayden did really good today."

This caused me to smile for real. "He did?"

"Yes. He wasn't nearly as fussy as he was the first few days. He actually played with some of the toys, he ate his meals and drank all of his milk, and he allowed us to change him without putting up too much of a fight."

My eyes welled up. "So he's getting used to it?"

"It seems so. I know it's tough to leave your child in the hands of people you don't know very well. But we try our best here to make our environment as safe and as welcome as possible."

I nodded. "Thank you, Monica. I appreciate it."

"Of course. Now, I have to get to my office, but I'm sure Kayden can't wait to see you."

I made my way to my baby's classroom.

As soon as he saw me, he started walking over to me as fast as he could. I met him halfway and grabbed him up in my arms.

As soon as I held him, I felt like everything was alright in the world.

If I could just hold and hug my baby all day long, everything would be okay.

Melanie

I picked up Jeremiah from daycare a little later than usual today.

Work was rough as hell - I couldn't stand these damn customers sometimes.

I work at a clothing store at the mall. You can only imagine the level of fuckery these people be on.

Honey, let me tell you: I almost had to cuss this lady out today.

She had me working with her for a solid half hour, picking out the perfect colors, jewelry, shoes, and a purse because she had a 'night out on the town'.

She nitpicked every single item I tried to help her find, then when we finally got everything together, she decided that she changed her mind and wanted to go to a different store.

People like that get on my damn nerves.

Like, why ask me for all this help and then not even buy anything?

Ugh. Anyway, I picked my son up from daycare and made my way to my baby daddy Jarvis' house to pick up my money.

I didn't really want to see him because his very presence irritated the hell out of me, but I needed my money so I had to do what I had to do.

I pulled up to his apartment and honked the horn.

He came out looking just as irritated as I felt.

"What did I tell you about honking the horn at me, Melanie?" he said.

I just rolled my eyes at him and held my hand out for the money.

He handed it to me.

I put the money in my wallet, then put my car in reverse.

"Wait," Jarvis said.

"What, Jarvis?"

"You not even going to say thank you?"

I cut my eyes at him. "For what? I'm not thanking you for shit you should be doing anyway."

With that, I backed out.

Jarvis was looking at me like he wanted to cuss me out, but I didn't give a damn. That nigga cheated on me and broke my heart.

I wasn't about to smile in his face like everything was good.

Nah, nigga. Just give me my money and take care of your son.

That's all I want and need from you.

Keisha

I had just come back home from my regular routine of Saturday mornings with my mom. We went grocery shopping together every Saturday morning ever since I first got my apartment. Well - I was sharing it with Rico originally, but surprisingly, he let me go with her.

That was the one thing he never took away from me - my relationship with my mom.

And ironically, it was that very relationship that probably saved my life.

I sat at my kitchen table, eating a bowl of oatmeal. I was trying to structure my meals in a more healthy way since Rico had always complained that I was fat…

"Stop it, Keisha!" I said to myself.

It seemed like no matter what I did, I couldn't get Rico out of my mind. I couldn't shake him.

He steadily invaded my thoughts, and all I could see when I thought of him was the look that he gave me when I told on him at the hospital. He looked like he wanted to kill me, and if he could have done it with his eyes, I would have been a goner that day.

Thank God for giving me the strength to walk away.

Even though I knew he was locked up and I was supposedly safe for the time being, I couldn't get it out of my head that he would be walking free very soon.

I needed a game plan for when he got out.

Just then, my screen lit up and my phone buzzed on the table in front of me.

It was Gina, one of the girls I had met at Walmart.

"Hello?" I answered, surprised to get a call from her.

"Hey, Keisha!" I could hear the smile in her voice.

"How are you?" I said, feeling so awkward. I honestly didn't actually expect her to call.

"Melanie is on three-way," she said.

"Hi Melanie," I said.

"Hey, Boo! What you up to this morning?"

"Nothing much. I just got in from grocery shopping with my mom." I hoped they didn't think I was a weirdo.

"Aww, that is so sweet!" said Gina. "Do you have plans for the rest of the day?"

"Um, not really. Why, what's up?" I could feel my anxiety levels increase. *What if they ask me to go somewhere with them? What am I supposed to say? How do I act? What do I do?*

"We were wondering if you wanted to hang out. Like, go get our hair and nails done and hit the club later tonight," said Gina.

"Oh… Yeah, that's fine."

"Girl, this is bout to be LIT!" said Melanie. "I set up appointments for us at my girl Shaneeda's salon. She said if I brought her multiple customers, she would give us discounts on blowouts. Girl, she is only charging us $35 a piece, and her whole team got skills. So you will be in good hands."

I chuckled. I already liked Melanie. "Wow; that is great! Thank you for including me."

"Of course, girl. I know how it is with money these days. Any way we can cut corners, we do. You have kids?"

"No…" I started.

"Girl, save some of the conversation for when we go out!" Gina cut in, talking to Melanie. "Keisha, can you meet us at the salon at 12:00pm? That's the time of our appointment."

I looked at the clock hanging on my wall. I had about two hours to get ready.

"Sure, that sounds good. What's the address?"

"I'll text it to you," said Gina.

"Okay, I'll see you guys. Thank you for inviting me."

When we hung up, I felt butterflies swarming in the pit of my stomach.

I had to get used to having friends again.

I mean, not that I've ever been a social butterfly, but the little bit of friendships that I did have were squelched by Rico.

I shook my head and brought my bowl and spoon to the sink to wash them.

I was not letting him get in my head today.

Gina

I dropped Kayden off at my mom's house, then headed to the salon to meet up with Melanie and Keisha. Melanie was actually paying the $35 for my hair, and I was going to pay for my own nails. She got us a discount for that too.

She was a little better off financially because her baby's father Jarvis actually paid her every week to help support his son. He also took Jeremiah on weekends to give Melanie a break.

Kayden Senior did neither of those things. The only thing he seemed to be able to do was flex on social media about how much money he was making with his new position on his job and try to throw his new little girlfriend in my face.

Fuck him and that dirty bitch.

I felt myself getting angry, so I made sure to take a few deep breaths to calm down as I parked my vehicle in front of the salon. Melanie's car was already there, so I parked next to her.

I didn't know what kind of car Keisha drove.

"It's a good thing Melanie is here first," I said to myself.

I got out of the car and gave Melanie a hug.

"Hey, Baby!" she said as she threw her arms around me.

"Hey, Mama."

"What's wrong?" She immediately sensed my mood.

"Nothing. Just thinking about Kayden Senior and his trifling ass, ugly ass girlfriend."

"Ugh. Girl… Tell me why I almost got into it again with that bitch Jarvis cheated with. I really want to fight her."

"No, Melanie. Don't do it." I said this, but I secretly wanted to lay hands and feet on the bitch Kayden Senior cheated with too.

"I know, but she keep trying me on social media. Slick dissing, then when I call her out, it's crickets."

"What she say?"

Melanie pulled out her phone to show me the screenshots.

I read them and immediately saw why Melanie was pissed.

Bitches mad cuz you fucked they baby daddy… Yeah I did it. And it was good, Roxanne had written.

"She better watch herself," I remarked.

"Pshht. She better fucking lay low," said Melanie. "She may be a keyboard warrior, but I'm really with the shit. Next status I see, it's on sight."

"Melanie…" I warned, but I really couldn't blame her.

Just then, we saw Keisha pulling into the parking lot.

"Oh - I meant to ask you: Can you hand me the money before we go in? I don't want Keisha to know you paid for me." I felt so embarrassed to ask, but Melanie been my girl since middle school.

She dug in her purse and discreetly gave it to me as Keisha looked for a parking space, then pulled into one.

"Girl, don't be embarrassed," Melanie said, reading my expression. "We all go through it."

"Yeah, but it's just hard." I felt a lump forming in my throat.

"I know it is, girl. And trust me: The only reason I am able to afford this myself is because Jarvis pays child support. I wouldn't be able to do shit if he wasn't."

A pained expression crossed Melanie's face and I knew why.

Jarvis had really broken her heart when he cheated.

Keisha got out of her car and walked up to us.

"Hey," she said, her eyes shifting back and forth, then she put her head down.

"Hey, Beautiful!" said Melanie, and gave her a hug.

I gave her one too. For some reason, I sensed that she needed it.

I saw her eyes well up a little when Melanie called her beautiful, but she blinked the tears back.

Hmmm, I thought. *I wonder what's up with that?*

We made our way into the salon, where as promised, Shaneeda and her team hooked us up. I gave Tricia, the girl who did my hair, the money Melanie gave me, along with a $5 tip. She really took her time to make sure that not one hair was out of place, even down to my baby hairs.

"Next stop is these nails!" said Melanie.

Like I mentioned before, Melanie had gotten us a discount for that too. I don't know how she does it, but she has a gift of gab with these nail techs.

I got the lowest cost mani and pedi, then gave the lady a $2 tip. It wasn't much, but I did what I could.

"I am starving!" Melanie said when we were done. "Where y'all want to go eat?"

I almost opened my mouth to tell her I couldn't afford to go out to eat too, especially since we were supposed to hit the club tonight, but then I remembered Keisha was there.

She had been mostly quiet the whole time while me and Melanie talked. I figured she was shy.

"That sounds like a good idea," Keisha responded. "I can actually treat, since you got us all these discounts, Melanie."

OMG! She is so sweet! I thought.

"Girl, you sure?!" said Melanie, giving me a glance before returning her attention to Keisha.

"Yes, definitely," she said, then she blushed.

"Wow, thank you!" I said.

We headed to Applebees. They always had good food at great prices.

Once we were done eating, we decided to head our separate ways, then hook back up later that night at the club.

Melanie

This bitch done used her last straw.

Almost as soon as I got home, I checked my notifications because my phone was blowing up while I was out with Gina and Keisha.

Once I checked my phone, I saw why.

This bitch Roxanne was getting a little too comfortable. She wrote another status about me - subliminal of course - but then one of the girls from my high school asked her if she was talking about Melanie (me). The bitch got froggish and said *yes*.

Then my cousin Sharmeka tagged me underneath it.

After that, people kept commenting on it, some of them saying that she better watch her back, and others saying that I wasn't going to do shit.

Sharmeka shut the naysayers down, of course. My cousin always had my back. None of them clapped back at her either, so nobody else needed their ass beat as of yet.

I decided to add my own comment to the mix, since niggas wanna have full conversations about me like I ain't there.

Roxanne, you got all this shit to say on social media, but when I confront you directly, it's crickets. You had your chance. I'm-a let you know right now: It's on sight.

I could not wait to see that bitch.

I contemplated calling Gina, but I knew she would only try to talk me down. I called Sharmeka instead.

"Bitchhhhh!" she said as soon as she answered the phone.

"I know. I saw it."

"So what you gonna do?"

"I just commented."

There was a brief pause as Sharmeka went to the status to see what I wrote.

"Aw, shit! You want me to ride with you?"

"Nope. I got this bitch myself."

"But what if she has people with her?"

"I don't give a damn. I'll beat those bitch's asses too."

"Melanie…"

"I don't care, Meek! This bitch been poppin shit for way too long, and I been letting it ride. Bitches think cuz I'm little that I can't fight. Bitch bout to learn the next time I see her."

"I hear you, but I'm just saying, be careful. If you want to pull up, I'll pull up with you. I just don't want you going alone."

"I understand that, and thank you. But I'm not planning on pulling up. I just plan to knock her on her ass the next time I see her. I'm sure it will be soon."

"Damn…" Sharmeka chuckled. "Well at least have somebody record that shit so I can see it. And if any other bitches decide they want to get in it, you already know how I do."

"I sure do."

"Okay. Keep me posted. Love you!"

"Love you too."

We hung up, and I ended up taking a nap after that. That food from Applebees was starting to hit me…

***

I woke up a few hours later ready to hit the club. I hopped in the shower, then threw on this sexy black dress and some stilettos. I did my makeup and touched up my hair, then I was ready to go.

I called Gina.

"Hey," she said.

"What's wrong with you?" I asked. Her tone sounded like it was off.

"Nothing. Just got into it with Kayden Senior."

I sucked my teeth. "About what?"

"Child support."

"Girl, you need to go through the courts. He's steady not paying you."

"I know, but I'm trying to give him a chance."

"Fuck chances. He knows he got a son."

"You talked to Keisha again?" she said, changing the subject. I knew she was doing that because she just wasn't ready to take Kayden Senior through the courts yet, no matter how much he deserved it.

"Not yet. You want to call her?"

We called Keisha to confirm that she was still going. She was.

***

When we got to the club, it was packed, but that's how I liked it.

"Hey, ladies!" this sexy dreaded dude said, looking directly at me when he spoke.

"Hey," I said.

Gina and Keisha also said hello.

"Can I buy you some drinks?"

He looked me up and down, and although he was sexy, he reminded me too much of Jarvis, who also had locs. It turned my stomach.

"No thanks," I said, and whisked Gina and Keisha away before he could say another word.

We went to the middle of the floor and started dancing.

Keisha looked so cute - I could tell that dancing was a natural gift for her from the way she moved.

I saw a few guys eyeing her too, but she didn't seem to notice.

Any time anybody caught her eye, she put her head down.

I wondered what that was about.

Gina wasn't much better.

Any time a dude tried to push up on her, she would dance with him, but I saw her turn down at least two guys that asked for her number.

She was probably still thinking about Kayden's corny ass.

I wasn't really looking to add any more dudes to my list either. I was already talking to Kylon and two other guys. I didn't feel anything serious for any of them just yet - I was mainly just having fun and trying to get over Jarvis.

The rest of the night went well. We stayed til about one o'clock in the morning, then called it a night.

"I really enjoyed myself with you ladies," I said as we walked to my car.

I had driven us, and Gina and Keisha had parked their cars at my apartment.

"I had a good time too," said Gina.

We looked at Keisha.

"Keisha? Did you have fun?" I asked.

She seemed to be distracted. She was looking around like she was suspicious or something, then when she heard me say her name, her head whipped toward me.

"Huh? Oh yeah - I had a great time."

I smiled. "How about we get up again tomorrow?"

"We can hang out at my place," said Gina, giving me a little look. I knew she was saying that because she couldn't afford to go out anywhere that cost money.

"That sounds great!" I said. "I'll make some fried chicken. Keisha, can you cook?"

"Um, a little bit," she said, then she put her head down. I wondered why she always did that. I almost wanted to reach over and lift it back up, but I didn't want to overstep.

"What's your specialty?" I tried to make her feel comfortable.

"Um, I can make some rice to go with the chicken," she said. Then she looked at me like she was asking if that was okay.

What is up with this girl? I thought, but I tried my best not to let my facial expression betray my thoughts.

"Rice is great! Girl, I will eat rice with anything! Gina, how about you make some of that fried cabbage?" I asked that because Gina's fried cabbage was BOMB, and because I knew she had the ingredients already at her apartment. She wouldn't have to go buy anything.

Gina smiled. "Yeah, I can do that."

"Yassss!" I said, throwing my arms around both of them. "We bout to bust down tomorrow, y'all! What time you want to meet up?" I looked back and forth between them, hoping they said they wanted to meet in the morning because my mouth was already watering, with my greedy ass.

"I can meet in the early afternoon. I get out of church around one o'clock," said Keisha.

I was kind of shocked that she said she was going to church - not because she seemed like a crazy sinner or anything, but I don't think I ever had a Christian friend before. *This is… different,* I thought.

"That sounds great!" I said.

"Right," Gina said, then she gave Keisha this look like she admired her.

I felt a little jealous, but I brushed it off.

I didn't feel any type of way against Keisha, but at the same time, she wasn't bout to take my baby Gina way from me.

Dramatic as hell, I know, but…

I just need to take my ass to sleep.

Keisha

I woke up the next morning actually feeling good.

I had a great time the night before with Gina and Melanie. They really seemed cool, and they made me feel so welcome...

I laid out my skirt, blouse, and heels, then I went to my jewelry box and got out a cute necklace and bracelet, topping the outfit off with my favorite earrings in the shape of the Cross.

I hoped the choir sang my song today - "Everything" by Tye Tribbett. For some reason, whenever I heard it, I broke down in tears.

I got in the shower, then when I got out, I applied some lotion before putting on my stockings, praying that the skirt fit. I had tried it on when I first bought it months ago, but this was my first time actually wearing it.

It fit.

"Thank God," I breathed, because if I had to change the skirt, I would have to change the blouse, and then the whole rest of the outfit, then I would have to change my jewelry, and my hair style, and I really wanted to wear my Cross earrings…

I shook my head to get out of my thoughts as I heard my mom's horn honking outside.

I looked at the digital clock on my nightstand. The bright red letters read 9:04am. She was a little earlier than usual, but my mom was impatient. She hated being kept waiting.

I quickly grabbed up my purse and made my down the hallway leading to my front door. I locked it behind me, then went over to the passenger side of her car to get in.

"Hm," my mom said, as she gave me a once over. "Took you long enough."

"Well, you got here a little early."

"Yeah, but only by ten minutes. Are you hung over from your night at the *club*?" She shot me an accusatory look when she said the word 'club', and her tone of voice displayed her disapproval.

"Mom, I didn't even drink anything."

"Good," was all she said.

She backed out of my driveway, then we made our way to the church, gospel music playing softly as we traveled.

When we got to the church, my mom looked me up and down, then back up again, pausing at my earrings.

"Why did you match that jewelry with that skirt?"

I touched my earrings. "What? There's silver in the belt buckle, and silver in the earrings."

"But it's not the same shade."

"Well, I don't think anyone will notice."

"I think they will. You should take those off."

"The earrings?"

"Yes."

"But then that would throw my whole outfit off!"

"Whatever," she huffed. "You never listen to me anyway."

We got out of the car and made our way into the church.

I glanced at my reflection in the huge window in the front area of the building, now feeling self-conscious about my choice of attire.

Mom was right - The two shades of silver didn't match.

It seemed like I could never get anything right.

Gina

I went to my mom's house to ask her if she could keep Kayden a little bit longer today so I could cook and then hang out with Keisha and Melanie in peace.

Not that I had a problem with my son being there, but he could definitely be a handful, and I knew he would want all of my attention.

"Hey Ma," I said as she let me in.

"Hey." She gave me a hug.

"Where's my baby?"

"He's in his room, sleeping."

Kayden had his own room at my mom's house. She loved her grandchild, I could definitely say that.

I tiptoed into the room and gave him a kiss on his forehead. He looked like a little angel.

I crept back out of the room to the living room where my mom was sitting on the couch.

"You're here early," she said.

"I know. I wanted to ask if you could keep Kayden for a few extra hours?"

She cocked her head. "A few extra hours?"

"Yeah. I'm supposed to hang with Keisha and Melanie today."

"Keisha? Who's Keisha?"

"This new girl that we met. She's really nice."

"Oh. Where's she from?"

"I don't know."

"Well, is she from here?"

"I don't know."

"Well, where does she live?"

"Ma…." I chuckled. "I have no idea. I just met the girl."

"Well, you need to find out because everybody ain't safe these days. You never know what people are into."

"Ma…" I fought the urge to roll my eyes. "She is fine."

"How do you know she's fine if you don't know her?"

"Ma… Stop watching all those detective shows. They got you paranoid."

"Hmph." She crossed her arms over her chest. "What time will you be back?"

***

After I left my mom's house, I got to thinking… I mean, yeah my mom is very nosy - she always has been - but we really *didn't* know much about Keisha at all.

When we hung out that day we went to the club, it was mainly me and Melanie talking and Keisha just listening… I shook my head.

Ma got me tripping.

My Bluetooth sounded with a call from Kayden Senior.

I rolled my eyes and pressed Reject.

I was not about to deal with him today.

I had to cook in preparation for hanging out with Keisha and Melanie, and I was not about to have nobody talking about my food cuz I ended up burning it after a conversation with Kayden Senior.

Melanie

I went to pick Jeremiah up from Jarvis' house, then made my way to my mom Faye's house to see if she could watch him for a little bit while I got up with Gina and Keisha.

I grabbed a sleeping Jeremiah up out of his car seat, then carried him up to my mom's front door.

Faye answered with a halfway attitude.

"So the only time I hear from you is when you want to drop your baby off with me?" She pursed her lips.

I sucked my teeth. "Ma, stop trippin. Can you watch him?"

She rolled her eyes. "How long, Melanie."

"Just a few hours."

"Hm. Why couldn't you leave him with Jarvis?"

"He has to work later on tonight and needed to catch some sleep." My heart panged at the mention of Jarvis' name.

"Hm," she repeated. "Well, I guess so. But you owe me a plate. What y'all cooking?"

"Some fried chicken, and Keisha is making rice, and Gina is making some fried cabbage."

"Keisha?" she wrinkled her nose. "Who's Keisha?"

"A new girl we met."

"Well, can she cook? I don't eat everybody's food."

"Ma. She's making rice."

"You can fuck up rice too."

I rolled my eyes. "I will bring you a plate."

"Make sure you bring me a big portion of Gina's cabbage too. That shit be hitting."

I faked a jaw drop. "What about my chicken?"

"Girl, I know your chicken is going to be good. I taught you everything you know."

"Yeah, whatever. I'll bring you a plate."

"All flats please."

"I know, Ma." I handed her Jeremiah. "And don't be leaving him with none of your trifling ass friends either."

She had turned to carry him to the couch, but turned back when I said that. "Oh yeah - speaking of friends, what's this I hear about you fighting some bitch off social media?"

I wrinkled my nose. "Who told you that?"

"Michelle."

I rolled my eyes. Michelle was my cousin Shrimp's nosy ass girlfriend. "She is so fucking messy."

"Did you fight her? Who was it?"

"That girl Jarvis cheated with. I didn't fight her yet, but she is definitely about to catch these hands the next time I see her."

"You better beat her ass too."

"You already know I will. She been asking for it."

Faye nodded. "I heard."

"Well, let me go get this chicken fried. I'll talk to you later."

"Okay, and don't be having me watch ya bad ass kid all day long either."

"Watch it now. That's still my baby."

"And I'm still your mother."

We stared each other down for a few minutes, then shared a laugh before I left.

Faye was so ratchet, and she got on my damn nerves sometimes, but she was still my mom.

Keisha

I pulled up to Gina's house feeling very nervous. I really hoped they liked my rice. I had watched it like a hawk as it cooked, ensuring that I didn't burn it and that there was no water left in the pot so it wouldn't be soggy. It was white rice, so I seasoned it with salt, pepper, and butter, but I wasn't sure if I put enough.

So then when I put some foil over the top of the pot, then the pot top over the foil, then put it all in a paper bag with strong handles so it wouldn't break, I considered bringing salt and pepper just in case.

Then I reprimanded myself because Gina probably had salt and pepper already. She was cooking too... But then I was thinking, *What if she ran out of salt and pepper? What if she ran out of butter? What if the rice was dry and tasteless and they hated it?*

I didn't want to ruin the meal.

I finally decided on putting the salt, pepper, and a stick of butter in a plastic bag and bringing that too.

If Gina already had some, I would look silly, but if she didn't and the rice was bland, I would be embarrassed.

I forced myself to take a deep breath as I fanned my face to keep my anxiety to a minimum.

I briefly considered going back home and telling them I was sick, but then Melanie's car pulled up behind me. I was stuck.

"Hey!" She said, getting out of her car. I got out of my car too, and gave her a hug. She went to her trunk to get the fried chicken, and I went to my trunk to get the rice and the bag of salt, pepper, and butter.

She had the chicken in a big plastic bowl with a lid. I could see that she had paper towels underneath the chicken for the grease.

"What's that?" she asked, pointing to my plastic bag.

"Oh…" I felt embarrassed already. "I wasn't sure if I put enough salt, pepper, or butter in the rice, so I bought some just in case. Is that too much?" I felt my pressure raising. I was starting to sweat.

"Oh - girl, that is so thoughtful! I'm sure you are fine though," she smiled. "Let's go in, cuz I am HUNGRY, Baby!"

I laughed, my anxiety levels decreasing and my heart rate returning back to normal.

"It's going to be okay, Keisha…" I said to myself under my breath.

Gina

Keisha, Melanie, and I had a great time over my house. The food was good, and we had a great conversation. I am really starting to like Keisha. She is really quiet, but when she does talk, you can tell that she is really intelligent and has something to say.

She seems really level-headed as well, despite the fact that she seemed a little nervous when she first walked in.

She is also very thoughtful - she actually bought some extra salt, pepper, and butter in case the rice wasn't seasoned enough. She had nothing to worry about though - it was some of the best I ever tasted, and it was just plain white rice!

She said she would leave the salt and pepper and stuff with me in case I had need for it in the future and I was so grateful because that's one less thing I had to buy.

Melanie left some chicken too, so I would have lunch for a couple of days. Blessings upon blessings, I tell ya…

I dropped Kayden off at daycare and he barely put up a fight at all. He actually waved bye-bye to me and blew me a kiss before he went to his toys.

My heart panged when I saw that because I knew he was getting used to being away from me.

I know you can't be with your baby every waking moment of the day, but still…

I got myself together as I exited my car in the call center parking lot.

I had finished training the previous week, and now it was time for me to start taking calls on my own. They were going to assign me a partner to work with and to listen in to some of my calls. His name was David. I hoped he was nice.

When I walked in, I immediately began to search the center for my new seat on the floor. They told us in training that we would have assigned seats on the floor, and that our cubicles would have our names on them. I went to Section C, where I was supposed to be seated, and almost immediately spotted my cubicle, feeling kind of nervous.

There was a guy sitting in the seat next to mine. I read his name sign and it said *David*, so I guessed he was my mentor. He was on a call, so I busied myself with sitting down and putting on my headset, turning on my computer, and getting ready for my first call.

When he sensed me sit down next to him, he turned his head in my direction, then did a quick double take before he turned away.

I wondered what that was all about.

He finally finished his call, then turned to me.

"Gina?" he asked, staring into my eyes.

I felt my heart flutter. This man was fine as hell! I did not mind him being my mentor at ALL!

"Yes, I'm Gina," I smiled.

"I'm David," he held out his hand for me to shake it.

I took it, and his hands were soft and warm, but firm and manly at the same time. This man was making me weak in the knees and I had barely known him for five seconds.

"Did they explain the mentorship process to you?" David was asking.

I was too busy staring at his lips, so I barely heard him, but I nodded anyway. "Yes, they did."

"Okay, they are supposed to be connecting our phones. The way they told me to do it was to have you take a call, and I listen in, and then I take a call, and you listen, then we discuss it after an hour. How does that sound?"

"That sounds good," I responded, reality finally sinking in. I was hoping and praying I remembered everything from the training class. I was not trying to look stupid in front of these customers, and especially not in front of David.

My first call came within a matter of seconds. I barely had time to think.

Of course, the customer had to ask me something that required me to navigate through the computer system to find her information, so I was a little nervous. David silently guided me as he listened in.

He leaned over the wall to my cubicle and pointed at the places on the screen that I was supposed to go to while I spoke with the customer. He was being very helpful, but I almost got distracted when I caught the scent of his cologne. Damn, he smelled so good.

When the call was over, I sighed.

"That was nerve wracking!" I said.

"You're a natural, Gina!" David smiled. "You did really good."

"I did?"

"Definitely. You followed all the screens and the prompts from the script perfectly. I think you got this."

"Well, don't leave me yet," I joked.

"Don't worry. I gotchu."

We shared a lingering stare, then David got a call, and it was my turn to listen in.

I watched his screen over his shoulder as he spoke to his customer with ease. The lady was a little irate at first, but David was so smooth that he calmed her down in no time.

When his call was over, we went back and forth a few more times, then it was time for us to get off the phones for our conference.

By the time the day was over, David had made me feel like I had been working there for years.

Melanie

Gina, Keisha and I were supposed to be hitting the mall today to do some light shopping. We went to a few stores, then hit up the food court to get something to eat. We settled for Chinese.

"Mm… This rice is to die for," I breathed as my eyes rolled back.

"Girl, stop," Gina rolled her eyes at me. "It is definitely not that serious."

"Whateva," I said, smacking my lips.

Keisha chuckled. "You guys are a trip."

"So… I have something to tell you ladies," I announced.

"What?" Gina and Keisha said in unison.

"I think I might cut Marvin and Tray off for Kylon."

Gina's eyes widened, while Keisha looked like she was wondering what I was talking about.

"For real?" Gina asked.

"Mm hm," I nodded. I turned to Keisha. "I've been talking to all three of them for a little while. They're all cute, but Kylon just has this edge. Every time he texts or calls me, it's a good conversation. I just feel like I have so much chemistry with him."

"Jarvis bout to be heated," Gina said, taking a bite of her egg roll.

I rolled my eyes at the mention of Jarvis' name. "Girl, don't even bring him up." I turned to Keisha again. "Jarvis is my baby daddy."

"Oh… Why did you guys break up?" Keisha asked. Then she second-guessed herself. "I'm sorry - I didn't mean to ask if you don't want to talk about it. I know we don't know each other that well."

"Girl, you good," I dismissed her fears. "He cheated on me with some bitch that's bout to catch these hands the next time I see her."

"Melanie…" Gina warned.

"Nope. Not today," I responded. "I didn't even tell you the last thing she did."

"It doesn't matter, Mel. We're not in high school anymore. You can't keep letting these bitches provoke you. Sorry, Keisha," Gina apologized for swearing.

"You're fine," Keisha smiled.

"I understand all that, but don't you want to lay hands on the chick Kayden messed with?"

"Don't even bring up that situation."

"I gotchu, but still. I can see it all over you that their situation bothers you. Her and Kayden basically do the same shit on social media. Somebody needs to start checking these hoes."

"They do, but there's a time and place for everything."

"And the time and place for me is on sight." I felt myself getting irritated. Gina was right with what she was saying, but I had already made my decision about Roxanne.

"This food is really good," Keisha said, sensing that our tension was building.

"Right," I said, taking another bite of my rice and letting my anger go.

Gina ate some more of her rice as well and I saw her relax a little from being tensed.

When we finished our food, we threw away our containers and started making our way toward the exit. As soon as we hit the parking lot, guess who the hell I saw.

"Well speak of the devil, and he shall arrive," I said, dropping my shopping bag to the ground and putting my earrings in my back pocket as I stalked up to Roxanne, rolling up my hair as well.

"Aw shit!" I heard Gina saying as I stopped right in front of the bitch.

"You ready to pop some shit now?" I asked, my eyes narrowed.

"Melanie!" Gina said, but I was already swinging.

Roxanne didn't know what hit her.

Hell, neither did I.

The only thing I saw was red as I grabbed her by the hair and drug that bitch across the parking lot, lumping her ass up with blows the whole way.

"Melanie!" I heard a male voice say, but I didn't let up.

I felt strong hands and arms pulling me away from Roxanne, then I finally calmed down a little.

"Melanie! You know you can get fired for this, right?"

I snapped out of it.

Tray was the one holding me back. He worked security for the mall - that was how we met each other. He walked me to my car one night after one of my shifts.

"That bitch shouldn't have been talking shit!" I spat.

"I know, but…" He looked at Gina and Keisha. They were both standing there. Roxanne had went back to her car. She was crying on the phone to somebody. "Can y'all get her home? I can cover for her as long as the other girl doesn't want to file a report, but if she does, she might give them your name, Melanie."

"I don't give a fuck!" I wasn't thinking rationally at all, and I knew it, but whenever I fought it took me a while to get back to normal.

"Come on Melanie," Gina said, looking like she was pissed.

Tray escorted us to Gina's car. On the way back to her apartment, we were silent for a bit, then Gina cut in with what I knew was coming eventually.

"You know, we just talked about this right before you fought her, Melanie. I know what she did was wrong, but we are not in high school anymore, girl. The fighting has to stop at some point."

"I said I didn't care, Gina!" I snapped. "She kept flapping her fucking gums. You shouldn't let your mouth get you into something your ass can't handle."

"I get that, but…"

"But what?"

She sighed. "Forget it. I can see that you're past reason right now."

"What the fuck is that supposed to mean?"

"Nothing, Melanie."

Gina turned the music up to shut my mouth. By the time we got to Gina's house where our cars were parked, I was back to normal. Gina turned the radio off.

"You good now?" She glanced at me through her rearview. I was sitting in the back seat.

"Yeah, I'm good, Mama Bear," I teased.

She chuckled. "Fuck you," she said.

I looked at Keisha, who was staring back at me from the front passenger seat like she was worried.

"Sorry you had to see that side of me, Keisha," I apologized. "I'm usually not like this."

Before I could even finish what I was saying, Gina burst out in a sarcastic laugh. "Girl, you tried it!" She looked at Keisha. "Do not let her lie to you. You can't take Melanie's ass nowhere."

"Aw, hush! I am not that bad!"

Gina just pursed her lips and cocked her head to the side.

"Okay… Maybe a little, but in my defense, she started it."

"And you beat her ass. Are you done fighting now?"

Keisha chuckled. "You two are so cute," she said.

"See! Keisha likes me. I didn't scare her off yet." I stuck out my tongue at Gina.

"Bwaaaa!" Gina laughed again. "And look at Tray's ass, trying to save you."

I laughed at that myself. "That was really sweet though. I'll have to thank him later."

"Eww!" Gina said.

"What?"

"You better not be 'thanking' him in the way that I think."

"Girl, mind ya business. I'm grown."

"Hmph," Gina said, causing Keisha to chuckle at us again.

Gina

All that stuff I was talking to Melanie must have been a set up for a test, because as soon as I went on my social media account, low and behold, what did I see?

Nobody but Kayden Senior and his stupid little girlfriend he left me for.

I really could not stand either of them.

But here I was, scrolling through both of their posts and pictures. Kayden Senior never took this many pictures with me - or with his son, for that matter.

I rolled my eyes. Speaking of my son, I needed to go check on him.

He had played all day at my mom's house, so by the time I got him home, he had fallen right asleep.

Once I finished checking on him, I went to the kitchen to grab my bottle of wine. I had been working on this same bottle for at least a week, but it definitely helped me to relax at night time. I poured a glass, then I decided to turn on this album by a gospel artist that Keisha recommended for me.

His name was Travis Greene.

I didn't listen to much gospel because I didn't go to church often, but since Keisha went every Sunday, it had me intrigued. I definitely needed to bring my son too, because I wanted him to grow up the right way. My mom went to church often too, and she was saved and everything. She was always telling me that I needed to go for myself and my son.

Maybe I would go with Keisha one day.

I scrolled through the playlist for the album on my phone. I had downloaded it the day Keisha recommended it, but I hadn't listened to it yet.

I was looking through the songs, and I saw one that said "Intentional".

For some reason, the title made me pause. I decided to listen to that one first.

I nodded my head to the beat as the song started, then as soon as the first line hit, I was hooked. Travis sang about all things working for his good, and how God was intentional.

The lyrics and the melody alone made me cry.

That song was everything.

While I was listening, I felt all my life struggles flash before me, and I felt like God was right there with me - like He could see me.

I never felt anything like that before.

When the song finished, I went to click to repeat it, but my phone started ringing with a call from Kayden Senior.

I sucked my teeth.

I can't have just one moment without him infecting it.

"Hello?" I answered with attitude.

"Where's my son?" Kayden sounded like he was drunk.

"Your son is sleep." I felt myself tensing up.

"I want to talk to him."

"I told you he's sleep, Kayden."

"Okay, well let me pick him up this weekend then."

"I've never held you back from doing that. You just never follow through."

He sucked his teeth. "What you mean, I never follow through?"

"When's the last time you saw him, Kayden?"

"Bae, who's that?" I heard his little bitch Alexa in the background.

"This my baby mom's," Kayden said to her.

"Well, hurry up and come to bed! Your *fiance* needs you!" She emphasized the word 'fiance' as she spoke, and it made my blood boil. Talk about a slap in the face.

"Fiance?" I said before I could stop myself.

"She's just playing," Kayden said, trying to talk low so Alexa wouldn't hear me.

"You wasn't saying that last night!" Alexa said, clearly desperate to let me know that she had the upper hand.

"Whatever. Good night." I hung up the phone in disgust.

Then I started kind of freaking out. Alexa was talking about being Kayden's fiance.

I remembered the night he had broken up with me. I had thought he was going to propose. Alexa called his phone while he was in the shower. I had answered and that's when I found out about them being together. He left me for that bitch the same weekend.

My phone was buzzing with another call from Kayden, probably wondering why I hung up on them.

I wasn't going to answer though.

He and his girlfriend had shattered my vibe enough for the night.

Melanie

Tell me why Tray broke things off with me?

I hit him up later on that night to see if he wanted to come through since Jeremiah was sleep. I wanted to thank him for looking out for me when I fought Roxanne at the mall, but he was not here for it.

"Melanie, I can't be messing with you no more," he said.

"Why not?" I responded.

"Because first of all, you could have gotten me fired for not filing that report. You lucky y'all fought where there wasn't no cameras. If the other girl would have filed something, we would have both been in trouble, but thankfully, she left right after you did."

"Okay… so what's the problem?" I stared at the phone as I urged him to continue.

"Fighting is not lady-like."

I wrinkled my nose. "Lady-like? Boy bye! Is fucking me the first night we met each other gentleman-like?" This nigga was not about to try to play me. Yeah, I know I shouldn't have fought her, but at the same time, his hands weren't totally clean either.

"That's different."

"How so?"

There was a pause as he tried to come up with some bullshit ass excuse as to why he was more of a gentleman than I was a lady.

I waited.

He had nothing.

"Look," he finally said. "We just can't see each other anymore."

"And that's fine with me. But at the same time, don't try to play me. You wasn't worried about me being a lady when you was all over me from the first day we met."

"You got that. I'll see you around."

"Bet."

I hung up with my feelings a little bit hurt because I knew there was some level of truth to what he said, but at the same time, I was planning on dropping him (and Marvin for that matter) for Kylon anyway.

Speaking of, a text from Kylon came through on my phone.

You up? he wrote.

I started cheesing. My thoughts of Tray dissing me were out the window that quick.

Yes, I am. Why?

Feel like some company?

Maybe.

How's little man?

My smile widened even more. Kylon had met Jeremiah by chance one day when I was bringing him to Walmart to get more clothes and things for daycare. He didn't trip at all that I had a son. He was playing with him and everything, and even bought him a little toy the next time we saw each other.

He's good. Sleeping.

I'm bout to hop in the shower, then come through in a minute.

Okay. See you soon.

Right when I was sending that text, a call came through on my phone from Jarvis.

I sucked my teeth before I answered. "Hello?"

"Why you always gotta talk to me like that, Melanie?"

"Like what?"

"Like you don't want to be bothered or something."

"I don't."

"Why can't we just talk about what happened?"

"There's no need. You cheated with that bitch, so we're done."

"Yeah, but you didn't give me no chance to explain or nothing, Melanie. You just dropped me like I wasn't shit to you. We got a son together. That don't mean nothing to you?"

"Not really," I lied.

Jarvis was right. When I found out he cheated, I dropped him. Just like that. Him telling me that completely caught me off guard because I thought we were happy together.

I had a little flashback of that day…

"Melanie. I have something to tell you." Jarvis was looking at me like he lost his best friend. I thought somebody died or something.

"What happened, Bae? Is everybody okay? It's not your dad, is it?" Jarvis' dad Reggie was heavy on drugs, just like my dad, Darnell. It was one of the things we bonded over.

Jarvis paused. "No, it's not my dad."

"Then what is it? Why are you looking at me like that?"

His eyes filled with tears. Seeing him that way caused me to tear up too. My mind started swirling as I thought of what it could possibly be. *Was he sick? Was it his mom?* He was starting to scare me.

"I messed up Melanie."

That statement brought me back to reality a little bit.

"What do you mean, you messed up?"

"I messed up," He repeated, but then he stopped again and swallowed a lump in his throat.

It was starting to dawn on me what he was saying.

"You messed up how, Jarvis?" I took a step back from him and crossed my arms over my chest, trying to brace myself for what I knew he was about to tell me.

"I messed around with this girl."

"What girl?"

He sensed the hostility in my tone, so he tried to backtrack a little. "That doesn't matter right now. What matters is-"

I cut him off.

"So you're telling me that you waited all the way til we had a son, til we're practically engaged, til right before Jeremiah's first birthday to tell me that you're cheating?"

It was starting to hit me, and it was hitting me in waves.

The nights he came home late.

How he was a little bit distanced from me lately.

How he had been a little more protective over his phone.

How he started deleting all his texts, claiming he didn't like 'clutter' in his inbox.

All the signs were there.

I just didn't see them.

I felt so stupid. So naive. I trusted him.

"Melanie?"

I didn't even look back at him. My ears blocked out everything else he tried to say. I started packing my shit right then and there to go over Faye's house. He kept trying to stop me, and even tried to physically restrain me, but I kind of blacked out. I started screaming and cussing at him and throwing everything I could find straight at his head.

When he saw that there was no talking for me that day, he left and said he would be back later for us to talk it out.

By the time he got back, all my shit and our son was gone over Faye's house.

Fuck that nigga. I never looked back...

"Melanie?" Jarvis was saying on the phone.

I snapped out of it.

"What do you want, Jarvis?"

"Did you hear anything I just said?"

"No, I didn't."

My tone was cold as ice, but I didn't give a damn. I probably hurt his feelings too, but I didn't care. I wanted him to hurt. Just like he hurt me.

"Melanie, it's been over a year since we split. Why can't we just sit down like two adults?"

"Because there's nothing to talk about. I've moved on. I have a new man."

I said those words to hit him where it hurt, because I knew he wanted to get back with me.

"A new man?" It sounded like it pained him to say it.

"Yes. A new man. One that would never cheat on me."

"Who is it?"

"None of your business."

"Who is it, Melanie?" He sounded like he was threatening me with his voice.

"Like I said, none of your business. But I moved on, Jarvis. You should too."

"I never moved on from you, Melanie. I still love you-"

"Yeah, whatever. Okay, bye."

I quickly hung up the phone before Jarvis could finish lying and telling me that he loved me.

I am never getting caught up in his bullshit again.

Kylon texted me right after I hung up with Jarvis asking me if I wanted him to bring anything with him when he came, but I was no longer in the mood.

I told him we would have to get up another time.

Keisha

I didn't hear from Gina or Melanie this weekend.

We spoke briefly through text during the week though.

I wondered if they still wanted to be friends.

Saturday I went grocery shopping with my mom, and she was going on and on about how I better not be hanging with any 'hussies'. She said they could end up bringing me down and hooking me up with another guy like Rico.

I assured her that Gina and Melanie were not anything like what she was thinking.

She assumed that they were because they invited me to the club that night.

Today my mom and I are going to church together, like we did every Sunday.

I got ready extra early in case she decided to show up before 9:15 again.

When we walked inside, my mom said she had to go meet with the ushers, so I was left to find a seat by myself.

I went to a row that had no one in it and sat at the very end.

I opened my Bible and got to the page in Genesis where I left off.

I had barely read three lines before I heard a male voice speaking.

"Excuse me?"

I looked up, and my heart dropped. I felt myself tense up.

"Is the seat next to you open?" he gestured.

I didn't know what to say. I nodded. "Yes, but my mom will be coming soon."

He smiled. "Well, do you mind if I sit here until she comes?"

My heart was beating wildly. "Um… Yeah, that's okay."

He sat next to me.

"My name is Mike. What's your name? I've seen you around, but I only know you as Beautiful."

My breath caught in my throat.

Did he just call me beautiful?

I touched my hair before I could catch myself. I had attempted to straighten it this morning, but it just wouldn't come out right, so I put it in a side ponytail. I put a butterfly clip in it to add a little flavor, but I didn't think it was all that.

"What's your name?" he repeated, and the way that he was staring at me made me look away from him.

"Keisha."

"Keisha, huh?" He said, and I liked the way it sounded when he said it. "Do you have plans after church, Miss Keisha?"

My mouth dropped open. "Huh?"

"I would like to take you out, if that's okay."

I froze.

Why did he want to take me out?

Was this a joke?

What was going on this morning?

Guys didn't find me attractive.

Rico said-

"Excuse me!"

I snapped out of my thoughts as I heard my mother's voice. She inched her way into our row and basically forced Mike to move over as she sat next to me.

My mother had big hips, so we were kind of squished together.

Mike moved over some more, so my mom moved over some too. Now, I was comfortable.

I was so grateful that my mother had interrupted our conversation when she did.

As cute as Mike was, I didn't think he would really want me after he truly got to know me.

Melanie

I was about due for a smoke, so I went over my cousin Sharmeka's house.

Just as I suspected, she and my other cousin Shrimp were already there.

"Hey," I said as I entered the room, immediately smelling the scent of what I came there for.

Well, I came to shoot the breeze too, but still.

"Long time, no see!" said Sharmeka. She had the blunt. She inhaled, then passed it to me.

I inhaled right after I sat down, then passed it to Shrimp.

"What's up, Cuz?" Shrimp said, his eyes already low.

"I don't even know if I should tell you anything anymore," I started in on him.

"What you mean?" he said.

"You run and tell everything to your messy ass girlfriend, Michelle."

Shrimp sucked his teeth. "I don't be telling Michelle shit. She messy by her damn self."

"So how did my mom find out I was planning to fight Roxanne then?" I cocked my head to the side at Shrimp, then I turned to face Sharmeka. "Unless you told her."

Sharmeka chuckled. "No, I ain't say shit. I'm just heated you didn't have nobody record it. I wanted to see that shit so bad."

"She probably found it out through social media," said Shrimp. "All y'all females post all your drama on there for the world to see. Michelle was telling me Roxanne made a Live video after y'all fought saying you jumped her."

"Jumped her?" Both me and Sharmeka said at the same time.

"When did she post this?" I asked.

"Now, who's messy?" said Shrimp.

"It's not messy if it involves me," I responded. I pulled out my phone, and Sharmeka pulled out hers too.

Of course, Roxanne had me blocked, so I couldn't see her status, but Sharmeka pulled up the video on her phone.

She turned up the volume and we all listened to Roxanne lie her ass off for a full five minutes, talking about, I jumped her at the mall with a pack of six bitches.

"Did anybody comment?" I said, heated when it finished playing.

Sharmeka rolled her eyes. "A thousand comments and counting, girl. Some people called her out on her bullshit, but others are feeling sorry for her lying ass."

"I should beat her ass again, and have somebody record it." I was stewing.

"What will that prove?" said Shrimp. "People gonna talk shit anyway."

***

When I got home, I called my dad Darnell up because I hadn't spoken to him in a while.

"Hey Baby Girl," he said.

"Hey Daddy."

"What you been up to? What's this I hear about you getting jumped?"

My forehead creased. "Me getting jumped?"

"Denise said she saw some video where some girl said she jumped you or something. You okay Baby Girl? Because you know Daddy will come handle some people for you."

I chuckled. My dad was so cute. It was moments like this that I relished in - moments where he wasn't high and we could have a normal conversation.

"No, Daddy. I'm fine. Nobody jumped me. I got into a one on one fight with a girl and I beat her up."

"Oh. What was Denise talking about then?"

Denise was my dad's messy ass girlfriend. If you thought Shrimp's girlfriend Michelle was bad, just watch out for Denise. It was a damn shame because she was at least twice our age and still getting in young people shit.

"Daddy, you know she never has all the facts. I don't know why you still messing with her."

"Aw, come on Mellie. Denise is not that bad. And guess what?"

"What?"

"You gonna be real proud of me when you hear this: I been clean for two whole weeks!"

My heart warmed. "For real?"

I could hear the smile in my dad's voice. "Yup. And I did it all by myself. I been telling y'all. I don't need no rehab. I got this."

"I am so proud of you, Daddy." I beamed, even though he couldn't see me. It had been a very long time since he had made it that long without using drugs.

"Thank you, Baby Girl. Well Denise is about to get off work, so I have to let you go. But you keep your head up and don't be fighting all these females. Stay safe for me, okay?"

"I will, Daddy."

"Okay, Baby Girl. I love you."

"I love you too," I responded, then hung up.

I reflected on my father's words for a while after we hung up.

***

Since apparently I was making my rounds today, after I took a hot bath and a nice nap, I decided to call Faye up.

"I been waiting for you to call me," Faye said as soon as she answered her phone.

"For what?" I was confused.

"I heard you beat that little bitch's ass the other day."

I felt myself relax. "Yeah, I sure did. I caught up with her at the mall. But guess what? Her corny ass made a Live video talking about I jumped her with six other bitches."

"Yeah I heard that too," Faye said. "But don't worry. I already set a few bitches straight about that."

"Who?"

"Some bitches was talking about it up at the salon while I was getting my hair braided. I cut right into their conversation and said 'My daughter doesn't jump bitches. She beats their ass herself. And if anybody wants to question her abilities in my presence, I can show them right now where she got her skills from'. Girl, from that point forward, those bitches said not a word."

Me and Faye shared a laugh at that.

My mom was crazy just like me.

In a way, it was how we bonded sometimes.

I understood her, and she understood me.

Except when she was getting on my damn nerves.

Gina

I felt like I was getting into the swing of things at my new job, but at the same time, I didn't like it. Literally the only thing good about it was the paycheck and my sexy coworker David.

We talked during our shifts and ate lunch together, but nothing more than that.

At first, I was thinking of trying to approach him, but I decided against it because I knew I wasn't fully over Kayden. I would hate to bring everything I was feeling against him and unleash it on David.

He seemed like a really good guy though.

Me, Melanie and Keisha were supposed to be hanging at Keisha's apartment this Saturday.

It seemed like the three of us were really hitting it off. Keisha was a really good balance between me and Melanie. I noticed that whenever we get into our little spats, Keisha is always the voice of reason calming us both down.

Plus I really like the fact that Keisha is in the church.

I really wanted to go with her one day.

I know I should just come out and ask her but…

"Gina?" I heard a female voice say.

I looked up.

She was standing next to my cubicle.

"Are you Sabrina?" I asked. She looked new, and they told me I would be a girl named Sabrina's mentor this week.

Yup - as much as I hated the job, I had been doing good enough for them to use me to mentor somebody just like David mentored me.

Unfortunately, he was out today. He had a doctor's appointment so he took the day off.

"Yes, that's me," she said, then she kind of cut her eyes at me like she had a problem.

"Is everything okay?" I asked her immediately.

"Yes. I'll sit down."

I watched her as she settled into her cubicle on the other side of me from David's cubicle.

Her response was kind of short, but I figured she must have first day jitters.

Because she definitely could not be getting an attitude with me.

Once she was settled in, I started speaking.

"So, did they explain the mentorship process to y-"

She cut me off.

"Yup. You listen in to my calls, and I listen in to yours. We go back and forth for an hour, and then we have a conference. Did I get that right?"

She flipped her hair - well, her wig - her real hair was showing around the edges - over her shoulder after she finished speaking, and I decided that I already didn't like this catty bitch.

I wasn't even going to tell her that she didn't have her wig on all the way.

Bitch should have checked a mirror or something before she came to work.

"Yup. That's right," I responded coolly, then Sabrina got her first call. She handled it well. She barely needed my assistance. But at the same time, it was a simple call - she didn't really even have to navigate the system.

Next was my turn. I had a complex call, so I had to navigate more deeply into the system to research information for the customer's account.

When I was finished, I turned to Sabrina to fill her in on what I had just done in case she got confused.

"So that was what we call a complex call," I began. "When a customer-"

"Yeah, you did okay on that call, but you forgot to repeat the customer's policy number back to her, and you didn't refer to her by first name only at the end of the call."

My jaw dropped in shock. "Excuse me?"

Sabrina whipped out her training manual. "It's on page 17." She actually took out a highlighter and highlighted the *script for customer's names* portion of the page.

The company had a policy where you were supposed to refer to the customer by first and last name to verify, then last name, then first name by the end of the call to make the company seem more personable.

"I'm aware of the policy Sabrina," I said.

"So why didn't you use it?" she countered.

"We all make mistakes," I shot back.

"I understand that, but when someone tries to correct you, you really should just humble yourself and let them help you."

This bitch…

This was about to be a long week. I could feel it.

***

I got home that day completely spent after a full day of mentoring Sabrina. If you want to call it that.

She literally nitpicked every single call that I was on, to the point that I almost snapped and told her to shut the fuck up.

Then she ended up going to the bathroom during our lunch break, and when she came back, her wig was fixed. I almost wanted to be petty and ask her how come she didn't catch that while she was so busy correcting me, but I decided to remain professional instead.

David texted me while Kayden was taking his nap.

How was the mentorship?

Ugh. I will talk to you about it tomorrow.

What happened?

Tomorrow. I can't deal today. I hope your appointment went well.

Right when I sent David that text, Kayden woke up from his nap. I could tell from the look on his face he was hungry.

I got him some milk and some level two baby food and began to feed him. He was growing so, so fast. It was like he was blossoming before my very eyes. My baby was walking much better, and even had the nerve to say over 30 words, and he was just about to turn two.

Between me, my mom, and the daycare staff, my baby was going to be right on track for preschool in a couple of years.

After he finished eating, I got out a little flip book his teacher had created for me and started pointing at the colors.

"Kayden, what's that?" I pointed to the first page.

"Red!" He looked up at me.

I widened my eyes in pride. "Yes, that's right! You're such a smart boy. Yay!" I clapped, and he clapped with me, smiling and showing his little teeth.

We went through the rest of the book together.

He didn't get them all, but I was proud of him nonetheless that he was already learning colors. My baby was a genius in my eyes.

Keisha

Gina and Melanie walked into my apartment.

I had made us some spaghetti and garlic bread with a side Caesar salad since we were hanging out today, and I had also gotten the ingredients for some hot fudge sundaes.

"Girl, it smells good in here!" said Melanie. "And your house is so clean!" She looked around at my pristine apartment.

I had gotten down and dirty to make sure my place was clean enough for my friends. I vacuumed the living room at least three times. I dusted all the glass tables. I wiped every smudge and speck off of the walls. I washed the dishes. I had even hand-washed and hung my curtains up to dry overnight so they would be clean.

I made sure to get some scented candles too, so they wouldn't think my house was funky.

I did everything I could to make it perfect.

"I know," Gina was saying. She was looking around in awe herself. "I mean, not that my house is dirty, but you are putting me to shame, girl."

I blushed. "I just wanted to make everything nice for you guys."

Melanie stared at me as I spoke. "Keisha, Baby..."

My heart dropped.

Did I say something wrong?

Why is she looking at me like that?

What did I do?

"What?" I said, bracing myself for the worst.

She touched my arm. "We understand that you are a perfectionist, but don't feel like you have to be all perfect around us. We like you just the way you are."

When she said those words, there was silence for a few moments.

I swallowed a lump that had been forming in my throat as my eyes welled up.

Then I let out a deep breath that I didn't even realize I was holding.

I nodded, releasing the rest of the tension I had been feeling.

Melanie's words made me feel free.

Like I was safe.

Like I could let my hair down with her and Gina, and they wouldn't find a way to criticize me.

Like I had really found some new friends.

"Thank you," I said, then we made our way to the kitchen table to eat.

We talked, laughed, and ate our food, then we had ice cream after.

Once we were finished, we headed to the living room to chat some more.

"Ugh! I am stuffed!" Melanie said, plopping down on the couch.

Gina stared at her as she situated herself on the loveseat.

I sat on a chair.

"Well, you did eat three plates of spaghetti, with ya greedy ass," said Gina.

We each looked at each other, then burst out laughing.

"Well, in my defense, it was slammin!" said Melanie.

Gina nodded in agreement. She looked at me. "Girl, she ain't lying. That spaghetti was hitting. That garlic bread too."

My heart warmed. "Thanks, guys."

"So… Miss Keisha?" Melanie sat up in her seat. "Tell us, do you have yourself a little Boo?"

I immediately felt self-conscious again.

"A Boo?"

"Yes, girl! I know dudes definitely be trying to holla."

"Well, not really…" I blushed as I thought of Mike.

"Ohh, she blushing! Gina, you see that?"

"Mm hm. I sure do," said Gina. "So who is he?"

"Well, I don't have a boyfriend or anything. But there was this guy who asked me out at church."

"Ooh, for real?" Melanie's eyes widened. "Girl, what he look like?"

"Tall, dark skinned, nice lips…" My mind went back to the day Mike asked me out and my mom blocked it.

"Have you talked to him on the phone yet?" said Gina.

"Have you guys went out yet?" said Melanie.

"No, neither. My mom interrupted us before we could finish our conversation."

"Oh no! That sucks. So he doesn't even have your number?" said Melanie.

"Nope."

"Well, we definitely have to fix that," said Gina. She pulled out her phone. "Does he have social media?"

"I think so," I said, like I didn't know. I was too embarrassed to say that I had been stalking his statuses since that day, but had yet to send him a friend request.

"Girl, what you waiting on! Take ya phone out. Now," said Melanie. She whipped her phone out too.

I pulled my phone out with shaky hands.

"What's his name?" asked Gina.

"Mike."

"Last name?" said Melanie.

"Williams."

Melanie's eyes lit up when she saw his page. "Ooh, yes girl. He is a cutie. Let's get you set up with that right now!"

"Yes girl," Gina agreed. She had found his page on her phone too.

"Go head. Send him a request," said Melanie.

I went to his page on my phone, then paused. "I don't know, guys…"

"What? What's wrong?" said Gina.

"I don't want to move too fast." My mind was on Rico and his looming release from jail.

"So you guys can start off as friends. Send him the request. I have a good feeling about this," Melanie said.

"How you have a good feeling just based on his page?" said Gina.

"Look at his statuses. He is basically Jesus in the flesh."

I had to chuckle at that one.

Mike did post a lot of inspirational quotes and scriptures, but so did a lot of other guys who turned out to be liars and cheats.

Rico was charming too, at first. Look where that got me.

"Girl, if you don't send that request…" Melanie warned.

"Okay, I'll do it."

I sent the request, acting like I was nonchalant on the outside, but on the inside, my stomach was full of butterflies.

"Aw, sooky!" said Melanie.

Mike immediately accepted my request.

My eyes lit up. "He accepted it!"

"Of course he did," said Gina. "Why wouldn't he?"

"He wants you girl," Melanie said, egging the situation on.

***

Later on that night after Gina and Melanie were gone, I found myself thinking of Mike.

Right when I was about to hop in the shower to get ready for bed, I got a message in my inbox.

Hey, Mike had written.

I definitely wasn't expecting that.

I wrote back. *Hey. How are you?*

Better now that I'm talking to you.

I smiled. *How was your day?*

Good. I went to work, then hung out with some guys from the church. How about yours?

Mine was good too. Cooked a nice dinner and hung out with my girls.

Cooked? What did you cook, girl? Let me find out.

The conversation went on late into the night from there. It ended with Mike asking for my number and saying he would call me the next day.

I definitely didn't want to move too fast, but even if we didn't end up together, I could see Mike becoming a great friend.

Melanie

Kylon was supposed to be taking me out on a date tonight, and I planned to finally put it on him. My only source of irritation was that Jarvis kept pestering me about who my new man was, and Marvin couldn't seem to comprehend that my lack of answering his calls and texts meant that I was no longer interested.

Hey Beautiful, texted Marvin.

"Ugh! Here we go again," I said, drawing out a short breath.

Hey, I texted back. My gut told me I shouldn't have, because it would probably give him renewed hope, but I couldn't take it back now.

Marvin sent me three more messages back to back after that.

How have you been?

I miss you!

Can we see each other today?

I sucked my teeth. "See, I knew I shouldn't have answered!" I tried to think of something to say back to him. I definitely wasn't seeing him because I was going on a date with Kylon, and there was no way I was breaking that.

Hey Marvin… Sorry, not tonight. I will be busy.

That wasn't a complete lie. I would be busy - with Kylon.

Marvin still didn't get the hint.

What about tomorrow?

I shot back a quick reply.

I will get back to you.

I held my breath as I waited for his response, hoping he left it alone. I sighed in relief when he wrote back.

Okay. I can't wait.

"Thank God," I breathed.

As soon as I set the phone down on the table from texting Marvin, my phone buzzed with a message from Kylon.

Hey. We still on for tonight?

I started cheesing as I read it, like he could see me.

Of course. I sent him a winking emoji along with the message.

Good. Don't leave me hanging again, now.

He was referring to the night Jarvis pissed me off.

You have nothing to worry about. Plus, I plan to give you a full apology for standing you up.

Kylon's response was even quicker than Marvin's.

Word?

I blushed.

Absolutely.

Well in that case, I'll clear out my schedule for the rest of the night.

I felt butterflies in my stomach as I sent my next message. This boy had me all in my feelings.

You better.

***

As promised, I was ready and waiting when it was time for Kylon to pick me up for our date. Jeremiah was with Jarvis until I had to pick him up the next day, so we would have the whole night to ourselves.

"Damn," Kylon said as he looked me up and down.

I was wearing a sexy black dress with some stilettos.

"I take it you like the dress?" I shot him a flirtatious grin.

"I love it. I almost wanna skip dinner and get straight to dessert."

I felt my neck getting hot. He didn't know what he was doing to me.

"Well, we better hurry up and get out of here then, because it sounds like I'm going to need all the energy I can get."

We made our way to Kylon's car, and he opened the door for me and closed it once I got in.

Such a gentleman, I mused.

We rode to the restaurant, chatting it up the whole way. Kylon was so cool. He was like the male version of me. I loved just talking to him and being around him.

Dinner went smoothly too. We stayed at the restaurant for over two hours, just talking and chilling and vibing. The more time I spent with Kylon, the more I liked him.

Then we decided to go to the liquor store to grab some bottles to take back to my apartment.

We went in the store together, laughing and joking around. Both of us were kind of buzzed from the drinks we had at dinner.

We were playing and flirting so much that I barely noticed that I almost bumped headlong into Marvin, who was on his way out of the store with a scratch ticket and a bottle of Henny.

"Oh, shit!" I said, covering my mouth when I saw him.

There was no time to hide.

He clearly saw me too, since I almost bumped into him.

He looked at me, then Kylon, then back at me.

He swallowed.

"Hey," he said, but his tone was barely intelligible.

Awkward silence followed.

"Excuse me," he whispered, then made his way out of the store.

I stood there in a daze for a couple of moments after he left.

"Who was that?" Kylon said. He was clearly still in a light-hearted mood.

"This guy I was talking to." I have no idea why I told him the truth, but I did.

He covered his mouth with his hand the same way I did a few moments before. "Oh, shit!" He repeated. "Was y'all serious?"

I shook my head. "Not really."

"Oh… Well, he'll get over it. Don't feel bad."

Despite the fact that Kylon was trying to make the situation light-hearted (probably because he didn't want to spoil the mood), I still felt like shit.

I felt like what just happened was a wake-up call for me.

I had been going back and forth with all three of these dudes, telling myself that I was just doing it to get over Jarvis, but I didn't really think about the fact that one of them could really catch feelings.

I decided right then and there that I was no longer playing the field. Hopefully things worked out with Kylon, but even if they didn't, I was only messing with one dude at a time from here on out.

Keisha

I got up kind of early Saturday morning to do my weekly grocery shopping with my mom. I had a little pep in my step because Mike and I had a great conversation on the phone the night before.

As usual, we talked late into the night.

It seemed like we never ran out of things to say to each other.

Mike was quickly becoming a very good friend for me. He was so easy to talk to, and he never tried to push me to do anything like Rico did.

We were supposed to be going out for the first time together tomorrow after church. I was kind of excited about it, despite being very nervous since this is the first man I have really talked to since Rico got locked up.

I was still on pins and needles about that too.

One of his female cousins, Tina, kept feeling the need to hang his impending release over my head.

She messaged me last night while I was on the phone with Mike saying that Rico was getting out soon, so I better be ready.

I almost messaged her back saying that I didn't appreciate her trying to threaten me, but I was no Melanie. I've never been a fighter, and I especially wasn't one after Rico.

He took all the fight out of me.

I stared at myself in the mirror, trying to see what Mike saw in me.

He was always showering me with compliments, saying I was beautiful, smart, funny… I honestly didn't feel like any of those things.

My eyes became blurry.

I dabbed at them with some cotton balls, because I didn't want to mess up my mascara.

I had made up my face today, something I hadn't done in a while.

I snapped out of my thoughts as I heard my mom's horn beeping outside.

"Dang it!" I said, glancing at my alarm clock before rushing to grab my purse and get out of the house so she wouldn't be left waiting.

It was 7:34am. Mom usually showed up at 7:30am.

I rushed out to the car, almost forgetting to lock my front door on my way out.

My mother started in on me as soon as I got in the car.

"Don't tell me you went to the club again last night," she said as she was pulling out of my driveway.

"No. I was…" I paused. I didn't want to tell her I had been talking to Mike just yet.

"You were what?"

"Nothing."

"Why are you wearing makeup?"

I shrugged. "I don't know… I just wanted to try something different today."

She stared at me like she knew I wasn't telling her the full story.

Then her expression softened.

"Well, it looks nice. It's good to see you getting back to yourself."

I felt myself relax. "Thanks."

We listened to music the rest of the way to the grocery store.

When we were about to get out of the car to go in, Mom stopped short.

"Wait - I forgot to tell you. Tomorrow after church, they are having a women's dinner. Did you hear the announcement last week?"

"No, I didn't."

"Me either. But they are leaving for the banquet hall directly after service. The fee is $30." She reached toward her door handle.

"Oh - I can't go."

She whipped her head back toward me.

"You can't go?!"

"No… I'm going somewhere else," I mumbled.

"Where else are you going? Cooking dinner over your new friend's house again?" Her eyes narrowed like she was accusing me.

"No… I'm supposed to hang out with Mike."

"Mike?" Her nose wrinkled. "Who is Mike?"

"The guy who was sitting in our row a couple of weeks ago."

"And how long has this been going on?"

"Nothing is going on. We're just friends, Mom."

"Is he why you are wearing makeup again?"

"No. I just wanted to do something different."

She stared at me for a long time, criticism evident all over her face.

Then her features softened like they did before, and I felt myself relax once again.

"Okay, Keisha. Just don't get lost in this boy, okay?"

I swallowed. "I won't."

Gina

I was over my mom's house chilling.

We hadn't had any mother-daughter time in a while, so we were giving each other manicures while Kayden played on the floor with his little toys.

"So, what's been up with you? How's work? How do you like your new job?" Ma asked.

I rolled my eyes at the mention of my job. "Ma, let me tell you: There is this new girl named Sabrina, and she is getting on my last nerve."

"Oh really? What did she do?"

"Are you kidding me? What did she not do? I'm supposed to be her 'mentor'," I paused on my mom's polish to use air quotes with my fingers, "But she steady acting like she is the one training me. Then she has the nerve to tell my supervisor that I'm not following protocol."

"Really? What's her last name?"

I shrugged. "I don't know. Why?"

"I might know her parents."

"No, Ma. Don't try to get in it."

"Well, if she is messing with my baby, I might have to check her."

We both chuckled.

"Ma, you not bout to be pulling up and fighting my battles."

"Listen Honey, I don't have to pull up. I can set her straight verbally."

"I just can't wait til they move her seat. I heard that they are switching her to a new team. Apparently, she tried to correct our supervisor on a few things too, and the lady got sick of her."

Ma chuckled again at that one.

"See? You don't even have to do nothing to her. Let the Lord fight your battles."

"Amen."

"So, when are you and Kayden coming back to church with me? The pastor has been asking about you."

My mom went to a really small church, where everybody knew everybody. Part of me felt like that was a good thing, because you always felt welcome, but on the flipside, it also meant that everybody was always in your business.

"I don't even know. We haven't been in such a long time."

"Well, how about tomorrow? You're not scheduled to work, are you?"

I shook my head. "No, I'm not. Okay, me and Kayden will come."

"Great. You need to raise that baby up in the Lord. And you need to get to know Jesus for yourself too."

My eyes lit up as her last statement sparked my memory. "Ooh, Ma! Have you heard of Travis Greene?"

She wrinkled her nose. "Who is that?"

"He's a gospel artist. Keisha told me about him. I downloaded his album on my phone. Hold on - let me show you this song."

I paused on her nails once again to pull my phone out of my pocket.

I went to the song "Intentional" and pressed Play. I had been listening to it on repeat almost every morning as I got Kayden ready for daycare.

My mom bobbed her head as she enjoyed the song with me.

Even Kayden started doing his little dance on the floor.

"What did you think?" I asked when the song was over.

"I really like it," Ma said. "Usually I don't listen to that new stuff - I like that old school Gospel. But I really like that song. I'm glad it ministers to you."

We stared at each other for a few moments as I took in the weight of her words.

"So, any new men in your life?" Ma asked.

A fleeting thought of David crossed my mind, but I shook it out. I wasn't trying to jump into anything before I got over Kayden Senior.

"No. I'm mainly just trying to work on myself while getting over You-Know-Who."

"That's good," Ma started waving her hands and blowing on her nails to get them to dry quicker. Once hers dried, it would be time for her to do mine. "Have you considered re-applying to school lately?"

I paused.

Part of me and Kayden's plan when we were together was to have me be a stay-at-home mom, but also to go to school and get my bachelor's so that I would be ready to enter the workforce by the time Kayden went to kindergarten.

Once we broke up, that dream was dashed. I lost my motivation.

"To be honest, I haven't even been thinking about it."

Ma blew on her nails again. "Well, you might want to get it back in your mind. You say you hate your job, right? I bet you could get a much better job with a degree. I always wanted you to go to college, Gina."

My eyes filled with tears. "Me too. But I just feel like I got so far off track with everything that happened."

"Honey, it happens to us all. But that's also what I'm here for. As your mother, I am always going to try to nudge you in the right direction. You might have gotten a little off track, but you can always get right back on it."

By the time I left Ma's house, I definitely had something to think about.

Keisha

Mike and I settled into our seats at a new soul food restaurant that had just opened up - Momma Jean's. It was literally the talk of the town - it was packed pretty much every day since it had opened the month prior, but I hadn't had a chance to visit it yet. Once Mike heard that, he said he definitely had to bring me there. So here we were.

"Wow, I really like how they decorated in here!" My eyes scanned the restaurant as I took in the environment. It really had a down-home feel to it. They had little booths along the walls, but then they had bigger tables in the middle of the floor that were set up to look like regular dinner tables, but just a little fancier.

On the walls, there were pictures of Momma Jean's family.

At the entrance, there was a picture of her family tree and a brief biography of her life and how she got the vision for her restaurant.

They also played a lot of old school blues and gospel music. It was a really nice atmosphere.

"Wait til you taste the food," Mike was saying. He had been staring at me as I took in all the sights of the restaurant. I blushed.

"What?" I asked.

"Nothing. Just sneaking peeks at your beauty."

I stared at the glass of water that the waitress had placed in front of me.

"Thank you," I said. I never felt like I knew how to respond when he said things like that to me.

"So, did you enjoy the service?" Mike asked, switching gears. He must have sensed my nervousness at his compliment.

"I did. It seems like the Pastor always knows what's going on in my life."

"I know, right! That sermon was LIT! What part did you resonate with the most?"

That question caused me to go silent again for a moment.

I wasn't sure I wanted to go there with Mike.

"What's wrong?" he asked.

"Nothing." I took a sip of my water.

"Keisha… You know you can talk to me, right?"

When he spoke, he stared directly into my eyes, like he wanted me to know he was for real.

And I'm sure he was… But I wasn't sure if he would still be so interested in me once he heard about Rico.

"I appreciate it," I started.

Then I decided to let him in, just a little.

"The part that resonated the most with me was the part where he talked about letting go of our past and moving on to the future."

The Pastor had spoken at length about that topic.

It definitely had me on edge, but he went in on the subject so heavily, by the time he was finished I felt like I had no choice but to let go…

Only I didn't know how.

How do you move on from something like what I went through?

How do you pretend that pain like that never happened?

"Keisha?" Mike was saying.

"Huh?" I snapped out of it.

"I was asking what part of your past do you feel like you have to let go of?"

His question was so simple, but for me, it hit hard.

I almost wanted to change the subject, but something told me I could trust Mike.

"I've just been dealing with… A bad break up."

I looked in his eyes to see if he would lose interest when I said that.

His expression didn't change.

"Why did you guys break up?"

I felt like I had told too much, too soon. I tried to backtrack a little.

"We just weren't good for each other."

"Oh really? Why not?"

Just then, the waitress came to take our orders, so I was saved from having to answer that question. When she walked away, I immediately took that opportunity to change the subject.

"So what part of the sermon did you enjoy the most?"

Mike and I kept the conversation light for the rest of our time at Momma Jean's.

When he dropped me off at home, he asked if we could see each other again the following weekend.

I kind of felt like we were moving too fast, but at the same time, I just loved being around him, so I said yes.

After I had taken my shower and was headed to bed, my phone buzzed with a notification.

I jumped to check it, thinking it was Mike.

It wasn't.

It was Rico's cousin again, saying that he was released from jail and that if I knew what was good for me, I would watch my back.

Gina

Ever since my conversation with my mom, I have been thinking about school really heavily. I really did just give up on it after Kayden left me. I felt like it wasn't an option for me anymore, since I was basically going to be raising our son by myself while he was out stunting with that little bitch…

I shook myself out of that thought process, yet again.

I couldn't allow Kayden Senior to consume my mind for the rest of my life.

It was time to turn over a new leaf.

Time to take my life back.

I called up Melanie, but she didn't answer.

I wrinkled my nose at the phone for a second, because she usually answered the phone when I called, but then I realized that she must be with Kylon.

They had been hanging out really heavily since they had sex.

I was kind of worried that she was falling for him a little too fast, but at the same time, she appeared to be happy, so I was going to just let her be.

I decided to call up Keisha.

We hadn't really spoken alone without Melanie yet, but I figured it was cool since it seemed like we were getting really close anyway.

"Hello?" Keisha answered.

"Hey!" I smiled.

"Hey. How are you?"

"Good. Listen, I wanted to talk to you about something."

"What's up?"

"So… Before I broke up with Kayden's father, I was planning to go to school. I was going to start off at a community college, then go for my bachelor's, and maybe my masters. But all of that was put on hold once he left me. Fast forward to now, I just had a conversation with my mom and she thinks I should give school another shot. Do you think I should do it?"

Keisha took a moment before she responded. "Wow, Gina! That is great! I think you should definitely go for it. When were you planning on signing up? What did Melanie say?"

"I was planning to sign up for this coming fall semester. I haven't told Melanie yet. I tried to call her on three-way, but she didn't pick up."

"Oh wow. Fall semester is only like two months away, right? And I'm sure Melanie will be proud of you when you tell her."

"Yeah, it really is only two months away. That's why I'm really nervous about it."

"Wow, you are inspiring me now! I was going to go to school myself, but then I…" She stopped herself.

"Then you what?"

"I um… I ended up getting caught up in a situation."

"Oh…" I waited for her to continue.

After a few moments, she cut back in. "But I'm really proud of you though."

I opened my mouth to ask her what kind of situation she got caught up in, but then an idea came to mind. "Hey - how about we sign up together? Since both of us were planning on it, but got sidetracked?"

Keisha was silent again. "That sounds good…" she started slowly. "I would have to think about it though. I'm not sure I'm ready to make that big of a decision just yet."

"Why not?" I pressed. Now that the idea had come to mind, it was sounding better and better to me. "It will be fun! Then we can take all of our classes together."

"But what if we don't want the same major?"

I paused. "Oh… Yeah. I didn't think about that part. Well, what major were you thinking of before?"

"Psychology."

"Oh my gosh - Me too!" I lied. I actually hadn't declared a major when I signed up before, but psychology sounded like a good option, and I really wanted Keisha to sign up with me for some reason.

"That's a crazy coincidence."

"I know, right?"

I tried to do a little more convincing as our conversation wore on, but Keisha was not budging til she thought about it.

I actually liked that - it showed that she wasn't a pushover.

At the same time, I really hoped Keisha said yes.

Then we just had to get Melanie on board.

Melanie

Me and Kylon can't seem to get enough of each other. He comes over almost every night after Jeremiah goes to sleep.

Ever since that first night, we been hooked.

The next morning, he tried to make it official, but I kind of curved him.

"Good morning, beautiful," he had said as we laid on the bed facing each other.

"Good morning," I smiled.

"You know I gotta make you mine after last night, right?" he said, licking his lips as his eyes traveled up and down my body.

It gave me chills. It made me want him again.

"Make me yours?" I wrinkled my nose, faking like I didn't know what he was talking about.

Kylon wasn't in a joking mood. "I need you to be my woman." He spoke in a low, seductive tone.

"Dang, all of that only after one time?"

"More like three, but who's counting?"

He was right - we had went at it at least three times the night before, and each time was better than the last.

I chuckled. "It sounds good to me, but I have to think about it first."

"Why? You still got feelings for dude from the liquor store?"

"Huh?" I wrinkled my nose again, but then I remembered that we had seen Marvin. That made me feel bad all over again. "No, not because of him. I just need to sort some things out in my mind first."

He stared for a few moments.

"Okay. I definitely understand that," he finally said. "But I want you to know that I'm feeling you. I don't want no other nigga having your attention."

I blushed at those words. Kylon's ass was about to make me change my mind just that quick. "Word?"

He nodded. "Word."

"Okay, well I'll let you know…"

My phone buzzed with a call from Gina, startling me out of my daydream.

"Hello?" I answered.

"Girl, what you doing?"

"Nothing. Sitting here thinking about Kylon."

"Ugh! Girl, he was not over your house again last night, was he?"

"Girl, you know he was…"

"Melanie! Y'all better be using condoms."

"Of course! You know I ain't crazy. What you think I am?"

"Pshht. Anyway, let me ask you something."

"What?"

"So… Keisha and I are thinking of signing up for psychology classes for the fall. The semester starts in two months. You down?"

My mind immediately began swimming. "Wait - you and Keisha - what?" I didn't know whether to be confused or to feel jealous, so I settled for both. "When did you and *Keisha* have this conversation?"

"Today."

I pulled the phone away from my ear, stared at it, then put it back to my ear.

"So y'all came up with the idea to sign up for school today?"

"Yeah… Well, it was my idea, but Keisha said she will think about it."

"And you called *her* first?" I felt my ears getting hot.

"Chill out, Melanie. I called *you* first."

"No, you did not." My voice was full of attitude.

"Check ya call log."

I pulled it up on my phone. Sure enough, I had a missed call from Gina.

"Girl, I didn't even hear the phone ring," I tried to play it off.

"That's probably cuz you was too busy letting Kylon play in ya pus-"

"TMI, girl. Anyway… So when we signing up?"

Even though neither me nor Gina were necessarily virgins - I mean, look at our sons - I was still a little embarrassed to talk about sex with Kylon. There was just something different about him. He has me feeling all types of ways.

"Well, Keisha said she would get back to me by next week."

I sucked my teeth. "And why we gotta wait on *her* before we make our decision?"

"Melanie, don't be acting like you still jealous. I already showed you I called you first."

"I'm just playing," I said, and I was. Mostly.

"Anyway…" I could practically see Gina's eyes rolling through the phone. "We can sign up as soon as Keisha makes her decision."

"Fine."

Keisha

Gina's proposal was really kind of spur-of-the-moment, but once I took time to think about it, it sounded like a really good idea. I had always done well in school, and I would have loved to go to college, but once I got caught up with Rico, the rest was history.

We started dating at the end of my junior year of high school, much to my mother's dismay.

If only I had listened to her.

I would have been much further along in life.

Not looking over my shoulder at every turn, waiting for Rico to jump out of the bushes to finish me off.

Sometimes when I have nightmares about him, I can still feel what it felt like to have him hit me. I can still hear the words of his verbal abuse, over and over again.

But it was time to do something different, like I told my mom earlier.

I told her about Gina's idea, and she was all over it.

Her perception of Gina and Melanie changed just that quickly, all because Gina suggested we go to school.

"See, that's the kind of friends you need, Keisha," Mom had said. "You need people that will help you move forward, not backward."

I pulled up behind Melanie's car at Gina's apartment.

I grabbed my purse and locked my doors before making my way to her front door.

"Hey!" Gina said, giving me a hug before I walked in.

"Hey," I responded. I looked at Melanie, who was sitting on the couch, focused on her laptop. "Hey, Melanie."

She seemed to be preoccupied with what was on her screen, so it took her a second to answer me. "Hey, Keisha."

I sat next to Melanie on the couch, and she scooted over a little.

I looked up at Gina, who was staring at both of us, but once I caught her eye, she smiled.

"Shall we begin?" she said.

I pulled out my Chromebook.

"Oh wow, Keisha. That is so cute!" said Gina. "Where did you get that?"

"I got it on sale at Walmart," I said.

"Y'all ready to fill out these applications?" said Melanie.

"Yup!" I said. I was starting to get the feeling like Melanie had a problem with me. She had barely looked at me since I walked in, and she was really short with her last statement.

I hoped I hadn't done anything to offend her.

I pulled up the school website on my Chromebook while Melanie pulled it up on her laptop.

Then I noticed that Gina was just sitting there watching us again.

"Gina, where's your laptop?" I asked.

Her face reddened slightly like she was embarrassed. "Oh... I don't have one yet. But I'm gonna get one soon, though!"

"Oh! I have an extra Chromebook at home. If you want, you can have it. I never use it."

Gina's eyes lit up. "Really?"

"Why do you have an extra Chromebook?" Melanie asked, but her question sounded more like an accusation.

"Oh, I..." I felt myself heat up as I remembered the day I bought it. And exactly why.

Rico had basically bullied me into getting one for him too once he saw that I was getting one. Once he got locked up, I had given all of his things to his cousin Tina so she could take them over her house, but I had kept the Chromebook - of course at my mother's urging.

"Well?" Melanie asked, breaking me out of my reverie.

"They had a sale that day." I tried my best to play it off.

"Well, I would truly appreciate it, Keisha," said Gina.

"No problem." I smiled.

"But for now Gina, we can share my laptop." With those words, Melanie got up and went over to the loveseat where Gina was sitting and sat next to her.

I was really starting to wonder what I had done to upset her.

Melanie

I know it might seem like I was being a little mean to Keisha, but she deserved it. She wasn't about to just up and take my best friend. Me and Gina got history, baby.

I knew I was going to hear Gina's mouth though as soon as I got home. Low and behold, guess who called me the moment I stepped foot in my apartment?

"Hello?" I answered.

"Melanie, what the hell is wrong with you?"

"What do you mean, what's wrong with me?"

"Why were you being so mean to Keisha? That girl did nothing to you."

"Well, she shouldn't be trying to take my best friend."

"Melanie… Nobody is trying to take anything. You know you can have more than one friend, right?"

"Yes. But you can only have one *best* friend."

"Girl… Ugh. What am I going to do with you?"

"Remember who you knew since middle school, and who you literally just met yesterday."

"Stop being dramatic."

"And why would you want to be friends with somebody that's just trying to buy you anyway?"

"What do you mean, buy me?"

"Giving you a damn laptop, Gina?"

"Melanie… I really think you need to get out your feelings about Keisha. She doesn't mean any harm."

"And how do you know that?"

"Because I just do."

"How would you know anything about her anyway? She says basically nothing when we hang out together. Unless y'all been having other secret conversations without me."

"Secret- Melanie, you need to chill. For real. Nobody is having secret conversations without you. We already went through this, remember?"

I lightened up. A little bit. "Yeah. Whatever."

"Are you going to continue to be an asshole to Keisha, or are you going to act like you got some sense?"

I didn't respond.

"Melanie… For real. You need to act your age. You are being really immature right now."

"Ain't nobody being immature, Gina! She just needs to know her place."

"Ugh. I'll call you later."

"Bet."

We hung up.

At first, I kept my little snooty ass attitude, but then I thought about Gina's words.

Maybe I was being a little immature.

After all, Keisha really hadn't done anything wrong.

I picked up my phone again to call Gina back, but my phone was already lighting up with a call from my cousin Shrimp.

"Hey," I answered.

"Hey. You heard what happened with your pops?"

My heart dropped. This could only be bad news.

"What do you mean, what happened with my pops? What's going on with Darnell?"

"He's okay, but he got arrested over the weekend for stealing from a convenience store."

"Oh my gosh…" This could only mean that Darnell was back to getting high again.

"I'm sorry to be the one to tell you, Melanie. But I felt you needed to know."

"Thanks."

"You okay?"

I paused. "Not really." My vision became blurred with tears. "This is literally never going to end, Shrimp."

"Don't think that way."

"Easier said than done."

Just then, my phone buzzed with a text message. I looked at it, and it was Darnell asking for $40.

"He just texted me asking me for money," I said.

"You know you can't give it to him."

"I know."

And so the cycle would begin, once again.

I went to bed that night feeling numb.

It seemed like no matter how many times Darnell tried to get off drugs, it would only last temporarily.

He just couldn't stop.

Gina

I dropped Kayden off at daycare, then I trudged into work.

Ma was right - I hated this job, and I had barely been working here a couple of months.

I couldn't wait to just get through school to get the hell out of here.

I made my way to my seat between David, the highlight of my work life, and Sabrina, my occupational nemesis.

"Hey, David." I sat down.

"Hey," he said.

I caught Sabrina rolling her eyes at us out of the corner of my eye.

I didn't bother saying 'Hey' to Sabrina, because I tried that one time and she had the nerve to try to correct me.

"'Hey' is not proper English. Especially not in the workplace," she had said. "This is not a casual environment, so we should instead say 'Hello' or 'Hi'. 'Good morning' would even suffice."

I swear, I wanted to knock that bitch's block off sometimes. I'm telling you.

From that day forward, I stopped trying to be friendly with her.

"Gina. I need to speak with you for a moment," Sabrina started, with her fake ass professional voice she always used when she was about to try to 'correct' me about something.

I stared at the ceiling and tried to calm myself before I responded.

"What, Sabrina?" I wasn't even going to try to pretend that I was open to this conversation.

Sabrina was unfazed by my annoyance. "I just wanted to share with you some notes that I've been compiling since we started working together. I tailored these to your areas of need, so I think you would find them quite helpful."

She held out a bunch of typed pages that were stapled together.

David had been watching our interaction while he waited for a call to come through on his line. He must have sensed that shit was about to get real ugly, so he cut in.

"Hey Gee. You wanna go to the caf right quick?"

The company allowed for us to take mini-breaks at times to go get a drink of water or go to the bathroom. You could only be gone for ten minutes, and could only take one mini-break on a four-hour shift.

I could definitely see that I needed mine now, despite the fact that I had just logged into the system.

"Let's go," I said.

We quickly logged out of our phones.

"David, that was quite rude. We were in the middle of a meeting!" Sabrina called after us. David just shot her a weird look and kept it moving.

As soon as we got to the cafeteria, David broke down laughing.

"Oh my God, how do you do it!" he gasped.

"What? Not strangle her?" I said, chuckling myself.

"This chick really pulled out a whole stack of notes."

"David… When I tell you…" I just shook my head.

"You are really, really patient." He stared at me, finally calm from all his laughing.

I blushed. "Well, I try to be."

"Maybe you could mentor me in that area," David said, and took a step toward me.

I took a step back, feeling the heat rise between us.

There was no denying that David was sexy as hell.

But I was not here to get a man.

I was here to support my son.

The cafeteria door opened, and a new looking guy walked in.

"Hey. Are you David?" he asked.

David looked a little confused. "Yeah, what's up?"

"Hey, man. I'm Shawn. I'm supposed to be your mentee this week. This chick named Sabrina said to come here to find you."

"Oh!" David covered his mouth. "My bad man. I forgot all about that. Let's get that set up."

"No doubt," said Shawn. He seemed like a cool dude. He looked at me. "Hey, how you doing?"

"Good," I smiled. "Nice to meet you Shawn."

We made our way back to the floor, where Sabrina's fake supervisor ass was shooting all three of us a look of disapproval.

"We have to get back on the phones, guys," she was saying. "It's supposed to be really busy today. Gina, I left the notes on your desk so you can take a look at them. David and Shawn - Good - it looks like you two have become acquainted. Let's get this ball rolling, guys."

I didn't even bother responding.

I just moved Sabrina's notes off of my keyboard and threw them in the trash at the end of my shift.

Keisha

I'm really starting to get excited about the prospect of going back to school. At first, I felt like I was moving too fast by jumping into such a big decision basically out of nowhere and so fast, but now I was really starting to warm up to it.

I always loved school.

I just got off track with everything once I met Rico.

He took all my time and all of my focus.

I didn't even see at first that he was basically taking me away from everything that I loved.

My friends, college, my mom (as much as he could)… even my job, almost.

It's crazy how you could be drifting so far from yourself without even realizing it until it's almost too late.

Thank God that Rico was no longer the ruler over my life.

I scrolled down my newsfeed, reading updates from all my high school friends and coworkers.

My heart almost stopped when I saw that Rico had updated his status.

I'm back, he wrote. *Bitches think they got the upper hand cuz the law is on they side, but I'm good. Better than ever, baby.*

I knew it was a terrible idea, but I clicked on his profile and saw that he already had a picture posted with another girl. I didn't know this one - she was different from all the other females he had cheated on me with when we were together.

I hoped that she didn't get sucked in by his charm like I did.

I should have blocked him, like my mom told me to, but I didn't.

My finger hovered over the Unfriend button, but for some reason, I couldn't bring myself to tap it.

What if he noticed?

His cousin Tina told me to watch my back - what if me unfriending him triggered him to come after me?

I shuddered at the thought.

I looked at my front door.

It was locked, of course, and thanks to the locksmith, Rico no longer had access.

But nowadays, that didn't mean anything.

I almost jumped out of my skin when my cell phone lit up and started ringing.

My anxiety subsided when I saw that it was Mike calling.

"Hello?" I answered.

"Hey. How are you?"

"I'm okay. What are you up to?"

"Nothing much. Just wanted to know if I could see you later on tonight."

I opened my mouth to say 'Of course', but I thought about it.

What if Rico saw us out?

That would definitely set him off.

He used to wipe the floor with me any time he even thought he saw me talking to another guy - friends, coworkers… One time even one of my male cousins. I had to show him a family picture to make him back off of me.

If he saw me with Mike, it could be dangerous.

"Keisha?" Mike was saying.

"Oh - I'm sorry. Um, unfortunately I can't go out tonight."

"Oh, that's cool. Are you free any other night this week?"

"Um… I don't know. I'll have to get back to you."

There was silence between us.

"Keisha, is everything okay?"

"Why do you ask?"

"Because it really seemed like things were flowing between us, but now I feel like there's a blockage."

"Oh… Well Mike, to be honest, I kind of feel like we are moving too fast."

"Too fast?"

"Yeah. I really think it's best if we just remained friends."

He was silent for another moment.

"Oh. Okay. If that's what you want."

"Yeah. I think that would be best."

"May I ask why?"

My breath caught in my throat. "Why?"

"Yeah. Did something happen? Did I say or do something to upset you?"

"Oh, no. You did nothing. It's just me."

"Oh, okay…" I could tell he was confused from his tone.

"Yeah." I knew I sounded like a fool, but I was doing what I felt needed to be done.

"Okay, well I don't hold you. I guess I'll see you in church."

"See you."

When I hung up with Mike, I felt like the scum of the earth.

I just basically broke things off with a really nice guy over Rico.

But if I pursued things with Mike, and Rico ended up seeing us…

I felt like I had no other choice.

Gina

I invited the girls over for a movie night, partially because I was trying to squash whatever beef Melanie had with Keisha, and partially because I honestly did want Keisha to open up to us.

Melanie was right when she said we barely knew much about her.

Hopefully tonight would change that.

"Hey, Girl!" I said, giving Keisha a hug when she walked in.

Melanie was already there. I believe it was because she wanted to make it a point to be there before Keisha to let her know she still had the "upper hand", but I honestly thought that she was being totally immature about the whole situation.

Who literally stops liking somebody out of nowhere just because they think you called somebody else before them one time?

I keep trying to tell Melanie that she's not thinking logically, but it all goes in one ear and out the other.

Hopefully that would change by the time tonight was over.

"Hey Melanie," Keisha said.

See, Melanie was going to have to stop doing that. Waiting for Keisha to speak to her first.

"Hey," she said without looking up from the TV.

Immature ass.

I rolled my eyes.

"Let me go get this popcorn popping, ladies. I also got us some sodas. Melanie, you want to order the pizza?"

"Fine," Melanie said, still pouting. Ugh, I wanted to throw a pillow at her head.

"And don't be ordering no olives on it either, either. I don't like all that weird shit on my pizza."

"Well, I like olives," Melanie shot back.

"Me too!" Keisha said, her eyes lighting up. She gave Melanie a look like she was desperate for her approval.

Melanie must have caught it, because she stopped being such a bitch.

"Looks like you outnumbered then, Miss Gina."

"Whatever," I said, but I felt myself relax slightly as I entered the kitchen to grab the soda and start the popcorn.

When I came back, Keisha and Melanie were sitting next to each other on the couch.

That was a good sign.

"They said they would be here in 45 minutes," Melanie said.

"They take so damn long!" I said. "I'm hungry now!"

"Well, I told you to order it earlier. It would have already been here."

"Yeah, but we had to wait to see what Keisha liked first."

I almost put my foot in my mouth when I said that.

I prayed Melanie wouldn't act up.

"Well, it turns out Keisha has good taste just like me, so there." Melanie stuck her tongue out at me, letting me know she was behaving for real tonight.

We started the first movie, which was *Girls Trip*. The pizza finally came when we were like halfway through it, but we barely noticed it had taken so long because we were so busy laughing.

Once it was over, I grabbed a stack of DVDs.

"So what do you ladies want to watch next?"

"Ooh, how about *Madea's Family Reunion*?" Melanie suggested.

I noticed that Keisha looked a little uneasy at the mention of that title.

"Keisha, you good? What do you think?" I asked.

"Um, yeah. That' fine," she responded, but she looked like she would rather do anything than watch that movie.

Against my better judgement, I decided to put it on just to retain the peace between Melanie and Keisha.

Once we got to the part where the fiance started beating Madea's niece, Keisha hopped up and said she had to use the bathroom.

"You want us to pause it?" Melanie asked, not seeming to notice.

"Oh no, you're good!" Keisha shot her a weak smile, then dashed off to the bathroom.

Melanie shot me a weird look, but she didn't say anything.

Keisha stayed in the bathroom for almost ten minutes.

I almost wanted to go and check on her, but she finally came out.

"Girl, you done missed half the movie!" Melanie remarked.

"Oh, it's fine," Keisha said. "I already saw this one."

She looked a little uncomfortable.

I wanted to say something, but decided against it.

We finished the movie.

"So, that was good," I said afterward. I was trying to find a way to ask Keisha what was up with her earlier.

"Yeah, especially when she hit that nigga with that hot pan of grits!" said Melanie. "I wish a nigga would try to do to me what he did to her."

"Right," I agreed, then we both looked at Keisha. She was dead silent.

"Keisha?" I said.

She was just staring into space.

"Keisha." Melanie said. She waved her hand in front of her face and that made her snap out of it.

"Huh?" Keisha said.

"You okay?"

"Yeah. Yeah, I'm fine." She swallowed.

"Is there something you want to talk about?" Melanie asked.

"No, I'm good. It's just getting late. I think it's time for me to go." She moved to grab her purse, but I held my hand up to stop her.

"Hey, Keisha. I don't mean to overstep, but you seem really bothered right now. Whatever it is, you know you can talk to us, right?"

I was trying my best to make her comfortable.

She needed to open up if something was bothering her.

"I don't really like to talk about it."

"About what?" Melanie prodded.

"Rico."

"Who's Rico?" we asked in unison.

A tear rolled down her cheek. "My ex."

"What happened with Rico?" I asked.

I sensed that she was finally going to open up to us.

"He used to do everything that was done to that woman in the movie to me. And much more."

My jaw dropped. "Wow…"

Melanie gasped. "Oh no! Keisha, I am so sorry! I didn't mean to make it seem like I was making fun or anything when I said what I said."

I felt like an asshole myself for playing it.

"I'm sorry for even putting that movie on if it brings back memories."

"It's okay," Keisha said. "You guys didn't know."

"So where is Rico now? Does he still try to contact you?" Melanie asked. She looked like she wanted to hit him.

"He just got out of jail. I've been really stressed about it."

"Wow," I repeated.

After that, Keisha opened up to us a little more about her relationship with Rico and some of the things she went through.

I could tell that by the end of the night, Melanie had completely got over her little beef.

"OMG, Gee! I feel like such a jerk now!" she said to me over the phone.

"Me too."

"Wow, who knew she was dealing with all that?"

"I'm just glad she felt like she could finally open up to us. That's a good thing."

"Right. Wow, you really never know."

"Indeed."

Melanie

After hearing about the shit Keisha went through with her ex, coupled with the drama with my dad, I was overdue for a smoke. I hit up Shrimp and Sharmeka and headed over to Sharmeka's house to relieve some tension.

When I got there, they both were already there, as usual.

"Hey," I said when I walked in.

"Hey," Shrimp and Sharmeka said in unison.

Sharmeka held out the blunt.

"Girl, you look like you going through it."

"Hell yeah."

I inhaled, then passed it to Shrimp before sitting down.

"You talked to Unc?" Shrimp asked.

I shook my head. "Not really. He texted me asking for $40, but of course, I had to say no."

Sharmeka looked at me like she felt for me. "I'm sorry you have to keep going through this, Mel."

"I know." I put my elbows up on the table and rested my forehead in my hands.

I thought I needed a smoke before I came here, but now I felt like I didn't even have the energy to do that.

Before I knew it, my shoulders were shaking as I let my tears fall freely.

"Oh, Mellie!" Sharmeka said. "Stop it, now! You gonna make me cry."

She handed the blunt to Shrimp and rushed over to hug me and rub my back.

"I'm tired of going through this shit, Meek! It's the same damn circle every time. He gets on, he gets off. He gets arrested, he refuses rehab. It never fucking ends. I can't do this shit no more."

"Shh," Shrimp said. "Mel, you gotta stay strong, you feel me? I know it's tough but you gotta believe Darnell is gonna pull through one day. Okay?"

"But when, Shrimp? He has been on drugs all of my life."

"We can't determine that. We just gotta keep hope alive."

I just stared blankly at the middle of the table. "Yeah."

Keisha

I stared at the message in my inbox from Rico.

Somehow I knew he would try to contact me.

Yeah... I'm out, he had written. *Looks like your snitchin ass plans didn't amount to nothing.*

Why wouldn't he just leave me alone?

He clearly had moved on with his little girlfriend or fling or whoever the girl was that he was posing in the picture with. Why bother me?

I contemplated whether or not I should write back or just block him.

As if he could read my mind, he sent me another message.

So you just gonna ignore me? Don't act brand new cuz you think you got this nigga to protect you.

He posted a picture from Mike's page under his message.

That did something to me.

He had no right to bring him into this.

He had already ruined whatever I thought I had going on with Mike anyway.

Just leave me alone, Rico. We're through.

What are you gonna do if I don't?

I'll call the police and show them these messages.

Snitching ass bitch. Always trying to bring a Black man down. Fuck you. You gonna get what's coming to you anyway for getting me locked up on some bullshit.

Fear and frustration coursed through my veins.

I was tired of this.

Tired of Rico.

Tired of him consuming my thoughts.

No more.

One more threat, and I'm calling the police.

The app showed me that he saw my message, but he didn't write back.

Thank God. He was done harassing me - at least for now.

147

Gina

I stared at the acceptance letter in my hands with tears in my eyes.

I felt like I had finally accomplished something in my life.

Even though pretty much everybody gets accepted into community college, I still felt like I was just one step closer to getting my life back on track.

I called my mom.

"Hey, Ma. Guess what??"

"What?"

"I got my acceptance letter!"

"Oh, Baby that is great! We gotta celebrate, girl. I want to take you and your friends out. Do you think their moms would want to come too?"

Well, that escalated quickly.

"Their moms?"

"Yes. I can't be the only old person there amidst all you young people."

"Ma, you are not old. You still got it."

"Excuse me, Honey. I know I still got it. I really just want to meet Keisha's mom."

And there it was. Ma was so nosey.

I rolled my eyes.

"Ma, if I invite her, you can't be going overboard with a whole bunch of questions."

"Of course not! I know how to have an intelligent conversation."

I chuckled. Ma was such a trip.

"Okay, I will ask Keisha and Melanie to ask their moms."

"Oh, I already know Faye is coming. She would never turn down a plate."

I gasped. "Ma!"

"What?"

"Why you talking about Melanie's mom like that?"

"Child, I didn't say anything bad. She just likes to eat. Heck, I like to eat too. We have that in common."

"Hmph. Okay, I'll ask."

"Great. Let me know what they say. And congratulations, Baby. I am so proud of you."

"Love you too."

Melanie

My screen flashed with a call from Gina, and I don't know how, but I just sensed that she had gotten her acceptance letter too.

"Guess what?!" she said.

"What?" I played along like I didn't know.

"I got my letter, girl. I am so excited!"

"Girl, I got mine too. Yasss!"

"My mom wants to take us out to celebrate. You think Faye would want to come? Ma told me to ask her and Keisha's mom."

"Oh, she wants our moms to come too?"

"Yeah. She was going on about not wanting to be the only 'old' woman there."

"Girl, your mom is a trip."

"I know."

"Well, I'm pretty sure Faye would want to come. She is not about to turn down a plate."

"Girl!"

"What?"

"Why you play your mom like that?"

"I'm not! Hell, I ain't turning down a plate either, but Faye really don't play about her food."

"You're crazy. Hold on, let me call Keisha and ask her."

My heart panged when Gina said Keisha's name. I was still feeling really bad about how I treated her.

Keisha agreed to go and said she would ask her mom too.

I came up with the idea to hit the club the same night we went to dinner. It was gonna be epic.

Both Gina and Keisha agreed to go.

I needed to shake some things loose, so I was even more excited than usual.

After I got off the phone with Gina and Keisha, I started getting ready for my date with Kylon. He suggested we finally go somewhere outside of my house since we had been doing nothing but sexing each other up since that first time.

"It's time we come up for some air girl," he had said. "I want to take you out somewhere. Show you off."

That line was so corny, but it turned me on anyway.

Everything about Kylon turned me on.

I felt like we just fit.

Like we were made for each other.

I had never felt this connected with another man before, including Jarvis.

Kylon and I still weren't official yet, but we were definitely moving toward it.

Keisha

I walked into the sanctuary with my mom on Sunday feeling very nervous.

Today would be my first time seeing Mike after breaking things off between us - if he showed up.

I halfway hoped I didn't see him, but another side of me couldn't get him out of my mind.

I wondered if he had been thinking about me as heavily as I had been thinking about him?

I scanned the room, but I tried not to make it too obvious that I was looking for someone in case I caught his eye.

I didn't.

My heart sank a little, but I decided to just focus on the service instead.

When it was over, my mom said that she was going to meet with the ushers.

Since I rode to church with her, I would have to wait around until she was done.

For a few moments, I just sat there staring into space. Then I decided to crack open my Bible. I was almost finished with the book of Genesis.

"Keisha?" I heard Mike's voice.

I looked up and saw him standing by the pew I was sitting in.

"Hey," I replied, feeling nervous all of a sudden.

"You mind if I sit down with you? I don't want to interrupt you if you are reading."

"Oh… Um… It's fine."

I may have sounded really hesitant, but in my heart of hearts, I wanted nothing more than to sit and talk with Mike.

He sat down next to me.

"What book you reading?" He asked, nodding toward my Bible.

My face flushed. "Oh, I'm just finishing Genesis."

He smiled. "That's great! How do you like it?"

"It's really good. I love the stories. But at the same time… I feel like there is a deeper meaning to them that I'm just not getting."

I didn't know why I messed around and told him that. Now he was going to think I was illiterate or something.

"A deeper meaning, huh?"

I nodded. "Yeah."

"Well, do you pray before you read?"

I wrinkled my nose. "What do you mean?"

"I mean like, pray and ask God to show you the meaning before you start reading."

"Um, no. How do you even do that?"

I was feeling more and more embarrassed by the second.

Apparently, I had been doing this whole thing wrong.

I had never prayed before reading the Bible. I just read it.

His gaze was penetrating. "Are you saved?"

I felt my anxiety rising a little.

"No, not yet. I'm working on it though."

"What do you feel is holding you back?"

I knew my face had to be completely red by now. "I just feel nervous getting up and walking down there in front of all those people."

"Well, you know you don't have to do that to be saved right?"

My jaw dropped. "You don't?"

He shook his head. "Nope. Getting saved is more about realizing who Christ is and why you need him than it is about walking down the aisle to the altar. You can walk down the altar and not ever truly believe in Him, or you can believe in Him right from your seat and be saved right where you are."

All of this was new to me.

I was literally hanging on Mike's every word.

He continued.

"If you want, you can be saved right now."

My heart dropped.

This conversation had gotten way deep, way fast.

"Right now?" I stammered.

"Yeah. If you want, I can pray with you."

"Oh - Mike, I'm not sure if I'm ready for that just yet."

I felt like I was in over my head with Mike.

He was clearly way more spiritual than I was.

"It's fine if you don't feel like you are ready. But I'll tell you what. I'm about to text you this link to an article that explains salvation. Promise to read it for me, and whenever you feel like you are ready, follow the instructions."

I felt kind of overwhelmed, but totally grateful at the same time.

Mike pulled out his phone to text me the article.

"Are you like… a preacher?" I asked. Maybe that was why he always shared all those quotes and scriptures on his page!

He chuckled.

"Oh no, not me. I'm just an average Joe. But Christ did save my life, and whenever I meet somebody that wants to know Him, I just wanna help. That's all."

"Wow, Mike."

He had no idea what those words just did to me.

I knew it was totally inappropriate, but I felt kind of turned on.

I hoped that thought wouldn't send me straight to hell, but Mike amazed me the more and more I knew him.

My mom came to get me from her meeting after that, then she dropped me off back home.

When I got there, I kept thinking about Mike more and more, and about what he had said to me after service.

He shot me a text later that night.

Keisha, he wrote. *I know you said that we are better off as friends, but I really feel like we have a strong connection. Is there any way you would reconsider us giving this thing a try? If we take it slow?*

I didn't know what to say to that.

Everything inside of me wanted to say yes, but at the same time…

At the same time, what?

Rico?

Was I going to let him rule my life forever?

Or was I going to move on?

It seemed like I had battled with these same thoughts a million times over, but I just couldn't seem to get over the hump.

I stared at Mike's message until the words got blurry and my screen went black.

Then I made a split decision.

Life was about taking chances, right?

Well, I decided that I was going to take my chances with Mike.

157

I shot him a quick reply before I could change my mind.

Yes. We can take it slow.

Melanie

Gina, Keisha, and I were going out to dinner with our moms tonight, then hitting up the club later. I planned to turn the fuck up.

I had so much on my mind lately with everything that was going on with my dad.

I just couldn't shake the fact that he had relapsed yet again.

I threw on a cute blouse and some dress pants, did my make up, then I was ready to go.

I picked up Faye on the way there.

Jeremiah was with Jarvis.

He was another problem - Jarvis, that is.

He kept pestering me about who my man was, then I guess someone saw me and Kylon together and told him who he was.

I got a call the next day with Jarvis sweating me, talking about he was going to 'beat that nigga's ass.'

"Boy stop. You had your chance and blew it. Move on. I clearly have."

"You never even gave me a fair chance Melanie," he tried to protest.

The dial tone was my response.

Hopefully that helped him get the message.

"Ooh, I heard this place was LIT!" Faye said as we pulled up to Momma Jean's, this new soul food restaurant that everybody was talking about.

Keisha said she had went there before with her little boo thing, Mike.

Gina and I had never been, but Gina's mom had went before. She reserved us a table.

We pulled up at the same time as Keisha and her mom.

Keisha was riding back to Gina's house with me to get ready for the club, and Faye was going to catch a ride with Gina's mom back home after dinner. They had taken separate cars.

"Hey, Babes!" I said to Keisha. I gave her a hug.

She and her mom looked just alike.

They were so cute.

"Hello," Keisha's mom said.

We made our introductions, then Gina and her mom came up to us and introduced themselves too.

We went inside to get our table, and we all made small talk as we waited for our waitress to come serve us.

That menu was LIT, baby.

They had everything you could think of - ribs, chicken, steak, pork shoulder, fried fish… And that was just the meats. The sides were even better. Mac and cheese, yams, potato salad… I was in Heaven.

My mouth watered just looking at the pictures of the food in the menu.

I was about to have that 'itis for real.

The waitress came around to take our orders. I settled on the steak. Faye got the fried chicken. Keisha and her mom both got ribs. Gina got fried catfish, and her mom got smothered pork chops.

"Thank you so much for inviting us!" I said to Gina's mom.

"Oh don't mention it, Baby. I am just so proud of you girls for taking this step in your lives. I'm sure all of us moms are," Gina's mom said with a smile.

"Most definitely," said Keisha's mom. "I got each of you a card." She reached in her purse and pulled them out, handing them to us.

"Well, damn," Faye said. "I didn't get you guys anything, but I do congratulate each of you too."

I could tell my mom was embarrassed by the look on her face, but she played it off pretty well.

We chatted some more throughout our dinner, which was delicious.

By the time we were through, I was stuffed.

That 'itis was hitting me on the way out the restaurant doors, just as I suspected.

"Girl, we might need a nap before we hit this club!" I said to Keisha as I drove to Gina's house.

"Indeed," she said. She looked very tired herself.

When we got there, the first words out of Gina's mouth were that we should catch a quick nap before the club.

Keisha and I looked at each other and laughed when we heard that.

Once we were finished with our nap, it was time to get sexy in preparation for our night out on the town.

I hopped in the shower after Gina and put on my sexy red dress with my black Giuseppe heels. Couldn't nobody tell me shit tonight.

Gina was wearing a purple dress with some black heels.

Keisha was wearing a black dress with black heels as well.

"Ooh, we definitely gotta get some selfies of all this slayage!" I said.

We got out our phones and began an impromptu photo shoot, alternating between sexy, serious, and playful poses.

I knew Kylon was going to flip once he saw me in this dress.

Keisha's little boo thang Mike had already hit her up once he saw the photos she uploaded to her page.

I thought that was so cute.

"Girl, he sweating you like that?" I joked.

She just blushed.

We hopped in Gina's whip then headed to the club.

It was packed as usual, which was exactly how I liked it.

I immediately headed to the bar.

"I don't know if you ladies are drinking tonight, but I plan to turn up!" I said, loud enough so they could hear me over the music.

Gina said she would have only one drink since she was driving, and Keisha opted out.

I downed three shots in a row because like I said, I wasn't coming here to play.

We headed toward the dance floor and started going in.

Almost immediately, dudes started coming up behind us to dance with us.

I was feeling really nice since the alcohol was starting to catch up with me, but I decided to have just one more shot to drown out my lingering thoughts of Darnell. That one shot turned into two, then when three. When I started toward the bar for the fourth time, Gina stopped me.

"Chill, Mel."

"What?" I whined.

"That's enough."

She was giving me this look like she was really serious, so I decided to listen to her.

Then I turned to the side and saw two greasy looking bitches stepping to Keisha like they had a problem.

Gina and I immediately walked over.

"Is there a problem?" I asked, making my presence known.

"I was just telling your little friend over here to watch her back," one of the girls remarked.

"Watch her back for what?" I demanded, my hands on my hips.

"My man Rico said she stay in his inbox. She better step back if she knows what's good for her."

"Rico?" I wrinkled my nose. "You mean the nigga that likes to hit on women? Don't tell me you are stepping to my girl over his bitch ass."

What I just said must have pissed the girl off, because she took a step toward me.

I didn't give a damn - I stay on ready.

Gina was right next to me.

The other girl was just standing there like she was ready to pop off too.

"Chill," Gina said, trying to be a peacemaker. "There's no need to spoil the night."

"Well, if she don't want nothing to go down, I suggest she get the fuck out Keisha's face."

The first girl chuckled like what I just said wasn't a thing to her.

"Yeah, whatever. But like I said, she needs to stay away from my man."

"And like I said, your man is a bitch. She doesn't want him."

The girls just walked away after that. But the second one kept looking back like she still wanted problems.

Keisha's arms were crossed like she was holding herself. She looked worried.

"Don't let those bitches bully you, Keish!" I said. "They ain't shit."

"Rico is here!" Keisha said.

"What? Where?" I looked around like I would recognize him if I saw him.

She nodded in his direction, and it was pretty easy to pick him out in the crowd. He was the one dude in the club who was shooting daggers in Keisha's direction. Plus he was standing next to the ugly bitches that just tried to punk Keisha.

"You good?" Gina asked.

Keisha shook her head. "I want to go home. I don't want to be anywhere near him."

Gina and I shared a look.

"We gotchu," I said, then we started making our way toward the door.

We were passing by the bar when Rico appeared seemingly out of nowhere and grabbed Keisha's arm.

She flinched in fear because he had caught her off guard.

I immediately stepped in between them and wrenched her arm from his grasp.

"Keep your fucking hands off of her!" I screamed in his face.

Gina stood on the other side of me so we were both shielding Keisha from him.

"What? Bitch, who are you?" said Rico.

"Unh uh, Baby. Bitch get your hands off my man!" the girl from before got between us. Her friend wasn't too far behind.

"Bitch?! I got your bitch, nigga!" I said to Rico.

He flinched like he was gonna hit me.

I grabbed a bottle from the bar and swung it as hard as I could against the finished wood.

I smashed it, but my wrist hurt like hell.

They made that shit look so easy in the movies.

I brandished the broken bottle in front of Rico's face. His girlfriend didn't do shit. Neither did her friend.

I had alcohol all over me due to breaking the bottle, but that was beside the point.

"Melanie!" Gina said, trying to stop me, but I was too amped up.

"You feeling froggish nigga?" I narrowed my eyes at Rico.

"This bitch is crazy," he said. His little girlfriend and her friend just stood there, not saying shit.

Just then, the security guard came over to where we were.

"Give me the bottle, Melanie," Slim said.

We knew each other due to the fact that I had fought in this club before.

"Nah, make this nigga leave first. He's trying to hurt my friend."

He looked at Rico.

"I ain't doing shit, man." Rico put his hands up. "She's the one with the bottle."

"Yeah, that's right, fold up like a little bitch," I spat.

"Okay, that's enough. Melanie, give me the bottle."

I stared at Rico.

"Not til he leaves."

Slim looked like he was getting frustrated.

"Can you leave, bruh?" he asked.

Rico shrugged and turned away, walking toward the exit.

I handed the bottle to Slim.

"And you can leave right along with him," he said. "I'm not breaking shit up tonight."

"We were already on our way out," I said.

Gina, Keisha, and I started making our way out. I was leading the way.

I was keeping my eye on Rico, his little girlfriend, and her friend, who were a couple of people ahead of us, just in case they tried anything.

We almost made it out the door, when all of a sudden, the bitch in front of me turned around and started swinging.

She clocked me real good at first, but then I started swinging back. Out of nowhere, two other bitches came out the woodwork and tried to jump in.

That only fueled my fire. I was full of adrenaline.

I pushed one of the bitches back and slipped off my heels with the quickness. I held them up with both hands, ready for action.

"Now what the fuck is up!" I screamed, but one of the bitches jumped on my back. I was so drunk I didn't even see her coming up behind me.

Amidst the ensuing chaos, I looked over and saw Keisha and Gina fighting Rico's girlfriend and her friend. Seemed like they were all coming out of nowhere.

I did some movie shit yet again and flipped the bitch that was on my back over my shoulders while the other two girls were still swinging on me. I dropped one of my heels in the process, but I still had the other one, so I started swinging that shit left and right, lumping those bitches up.

I have no idea how I was doing it, but I was handling all three of those bitches all at once.

The only thing my mind kept telling me was to keep on moving, so that's what I did.

I didn't stop moving, so they couldn't get an edge over me.

Security guards swarmed us to break it up, and one of them wrenched my other heel from my grasp.

They started pulling us out the doors of the club to keep us from further fucking up their establishment.

Once we got outside, one of the bitches got free and tried to rush me, but I picked up a bottle from the ground and threw it at her head.

She ducked in the nick of time, so I missed her, but then the security guard grabbed her up again.

"Calm the fuck down! Calm the fuck down!" Slim was screaming.

He had been screaming that over and over again, but I was so full of adrenaline, I never even heard him.

Then we heard sirens.

They held us til the police came, then me and the three bitches that I had been fighting ended up getting arrested. The other two girls that fought Gina and Keisha had gotten away. Nobody snitched on Gina and Keisha, though they were right there with me when the police cuffed me.

Of course, Rico's ass had dipped some time during the commotion.

This was the most wild night of my life to date.

I was barefoot and drenched in alcohol, riding in the back of a fucking police cruiser.

My second time being arrested for some fighting shit.

Gina

I was livid.

Everything had happened so fast at that club - I barely knew what hit me.

One minute, we were laughing and having fun, and the next, that chick was all in Keisha's face, then all I saw was bottles and fists flying, then Melanie ended up getting arrested.

OMG. This night was not supposed to end this way.

We pulled up to the police station to bail Melanie out.

They told us it would be a little bit of a wait before we would know exactly how much it would cost to get her out.

Of course, I didn't have any money, but I was prepared to overdraw my account for my friend. I also texted Melanie's cousins Shrimp and Sharmeka, and her mom Faye. They each said they would put in on whatever the cost was too.

That alleviated the burden a lot.

"Of course, I will help out too," Keisha said when I told her what Melanie's family said.

She looked how I felt - tired, frustrated, and just worn out in general.

"I am so sorry all this happened tonight," I said.

"Me too."

"That was so crazy."

"I know. I've literally never been in a fight before tonight. But I appreciate you guys for standing up for me."

"Girl, it looked like you was standing up for yourself just fine with the way you was swinging on home girl!"

We both chuckled.

Just then, we saw a familiar face - Melanie's boo, Kylon. He had walked in with some other guy.

"Hey, Gina." He said, giving me a strange look. "What are you doing here?"

"Bailing your girlfriend out," I replied, giving him a look. Then I thought about it. I hoped that Melanie wouldn't get mad at me for telling him that.

"Melanie is in here?" He looked shocked.

"We got into a fight at the club."

"Oh, shit. That's why she didn't answer my text. How much is her bail?"

"We don't know yet. Wait, who are you bailing out?"

"Oh, I just came here with my boy, Trell." He nodded his head toward the guy he walked in with, who was talking to a bail bondsman. "He's bailing out his girl."

"From the same incident?" I immediately felt myself getting defensive.

He shook his head. "Different club from the one y'all went to."

"Oh. Okay," I relaxed. "Wait - I'm being rude. This is Keisha."

I introduced Keisha and Kylon.

Finally, the bail bondsman had an amount for Melanie's release.

Once he heard that it was $500, Kylon said he would pay it.

My jaw dropped. "You sure?"

"Yeah," he nodded like there was no doubt in his mind. "I got it."

And he really went and paid the money too.

Melanie might have her a keeper.

We had to wait a little longer for them to actually let Melanie out, but when they did, she looked completely shocked to see Kylon.

"Oh my God, what are you doing here?" she said, hugging him.

Kylon looked her up and down. "You getting into all kinds of trouble without me, I see."

"Shut up," she said, pushing his head.

Then she looked down at her ripped dress and her bare feet.

"OMG! Y'all can't have me out here looking ratchet like this. I am so embarrassed, Kylon."

"Oh quit it. You look beautiful," Kylon said.

She cocked her head to the side and pursed her lips.

"What?" Kylon chuckled.

"Beautiful?"

"A little rough around the edges, but nothing a little comb to the head wouldn't fix."

With that, we all burst out laughing as Melanie swatted at Kylon.

He ducked all of her hits, then pulled her in for a bear hug.

"Awww!" Keisha and I said.

Those two were so cute.

Epilogue

Keisha

Rico hasn't said anything to me since that night, thank God.

Mike and I have been hanging out a lot, however, which has been great.

I finally broke down and told him about Rico.

Surprisingly, he was very understanding.

I also ended up reading that article that he texted me before the big blow-up at the club.

It provided a clear explanation of what it meant to be saved.

By the time I finished it, I felt like I was ready to give my life to Christ.

I got down on my knees right then and there, and poured my heart out to God.

I prayed like I had never prayed before, asking Him to come into my life and save me from my sins.

After the prayer, I felt brand new.

Like something changed inside of me.

I immediately called my mom and told her what I had done.

She was skeptical at first, because I hadn't went down to the altar at the church.

"I'm not trying to say you're not saved, Keisha," she said. "But what you did was unconventional, is all."

I understood where she was coming from, but at the same time, I knew what happened inside of me.

I went back and started reading the book of Genesis again, and it was like a light bulb had went off in my brain or something.

I was able to make sense of what I read before, but now when I read it, it was so profound.

I got through half the book in one night, and the next night, I finished it.

I was hungry for more, so I started Exodus the very next night.

I told Mike I got saved too. He was so happy for me.

So were Gina and Melanie.

I was so glad to truly meet some friends.

Melanie

Shortly after that night at the club, Darnell called me up and told me he was back to being clean again. He had made it four days when we spoke.

I urged him to just go to rehab, but he said he could handle it himself.

I tried to protest, but he had already made up his mind.

So I just left it alone.

Like I said before, that night was the craziest night of my life to date. At my court date, they wanted to give me a month in jail, but since I had a son, I had just enrolled in school, and I was working full-time, the public defender was able to work out a deal with the judge so that I would only do four weekends in jail and have three months of probation, along with 100 hours of community service.

I had no idea how the hell I was gonna swing all that while I was just getting started with school, but I kept my mouth shut and took the deal.

Thankfully, me and my supervisor were really cool, so she let me switch my schedule to Monday through Friday for the weekends I would be in jail.

Of course, Jarvis would be keeping Jeremiah on the weekends as usual, so he wouldn't have a reason to miss his mom.

We also kind of made up - me and Jarvis. I told him I forgave him for cheating, but I would appreciate it if he just left me alone about Kylon.

He said he agreed with me. We will see how long that lasts.

Speaking of Kylon, things are going really well with him.

We're finally official, and we are thinking of moving in together.

A part of me feels like we are moving way too fast, but another part of me feels like I might be in love.

Oh well. I guess we will see.

Gina

I can't believe we are actually doing it. We are really starting school.

Keisha, Melanie, and I made a pact that we were in this together. We planned to take all of our classes on the same schedule and to work together to study, etc.

It felt so surreal.

Work was going slightly better. Thankfully, Sabrina was moved to another team, so I don't have to sit next to her or hear her annoying ass mouth any longer.

At least I hope.

Me and David are still cool, but he hasn't tried to say anything to me as of yet.

I'm kind of hoping he keeps it that way, because he is very tempting, and I just want to focus on my son and school.

My goal is to go straight through school with my girls, getting our associate's, bachelor's, and possibly our masters, and getting me and my son out of poverty.

I wished that things would have worked out with Kayden Senior, but it seems like he really moved on with that girl Alexa he was with, so I have no choice but to move on as well.

Want to know what happens next with these ladies?

Check out the first official book in the series: For My Good: My Baby Daddy Ain't Ish (Gina's story).

Before you go…

I hope you enjoyed reading about Gina, Keisha, and Melanie. If you would like to join a dynamic group of readers and authors where we discuss books, life, and other things in between, check out Tanisha Stewart Readers (Facebook).

If you would like to read more books by Tanisha Stewart, just turn the page!

Tanisha Stewart's Books

Even Me Series

Even Me

Even Me, The Sequel

Even Me, Full Circle

When Things Go Series

When Things Go Left

When Things Get Real

When Things Go Right

For My Good Series

For My Good: The Prequel

For My Good: My Baby Daddy Ain't Ish

For My Good: I Waited, He Cheated

For My Good: Torn Between The Two

For My Good: You Broke My Trust

For My Good: Better or Worse

For My Good: Love and Respect

Betrayed Series

Betrayed By My So-Called Friend

Betrayed By My So-Called Friend, Part 2

Betrayed 3: Camaiyah's Redemption

Betrayed Series: Special Edition

Standalones

A Husband, A Boyfriend, & a Side Dude

In Love With My Uber Driver

You Left Me At The Altar

Where. Is. Haseem?! A Romantic-Suspense Comedy

Caught Up With The 'Rona: An Urban Sci-Fi Thriller

#DOLO: An Awkward, Non-Romantic Journey Through Singlehood